YES

YES

Screenplay and Notes by Sally Potter

Introductions by
John Berger and Pankaj Mishra

Q&A with Sally Potter
and Joan Allen

Newmarket Press • New York

YES screenplay by Sally Potter © 2005 GreeneStreet Films LLC and UK Film Council

The original five-minute script, foreword, and Q&A with Sally Potter and Joan Allen © 2005 Sally Potter

"A Letter" © 2005 John Berger

Introduction © 2005 Pankaj Mishra

Photographs page vi, 1-22, 24, and 27 © 2005 Nicola Dove, Eyebox Photographs 23, 25, 26, and 28 © 2005 Gautier Deblonde

This book is published in the United States of America.

First Edition
ISBN 1-55704-666-2 (paperback)
ISBN 1-55704-667-0 (hardcover)

10 9 8 7 6 5 4 3 2 1

Library of Congress Cataloging-in-Publication Data
Potter, Sally.
  Yes : screenplay and notes / Sally Potter.—1st ed.
    p. cm.
  ISBN 1-55704-666-2 (pbk. : alk. paper)
  1. Yes (Motion picture : 2004) I. Title.
  PN1997.2.Y47P68 2005
  791.43'72—dc22
                                        2005006889

QUANTITY PURCHASES
Companies, professional groups, clubs, and other organizations may qualify for special terms when ordering quantities of this title. For information, write Special Sales Department, Newmarket Press, 18 East 48th Street, New York, NY 10017; call (212) 832-3575; fax (212) 832-3629; or e-mail info@newmarketpress.com.

www.yesthemovie.com
www.sallypotter.com
www.newmarketpress.com

Manufactured in the United States of America.

Contents

Foreword

by Sally Potter

YES started life as a five-minute film in which two lovers—a Middle Eastern man (from Beirut) and an Irish woman (from Belfast)—are each having an imaginary argument with the other as they walk towards a meeting both think will be their last, for the relationship seems to be coming to a bitter end. However by the time they meet they have each privately resolved their conflict and re-found their love, desire, and respect for each other.

This short film, set in Paris, became the starting point for a full-length screenplay, centered on the two characters, but now set in London, Belfast, Beirut, and Havana. The story expanded to include other key relationships, the protagonists' workplaces and a cleaner whose monologues functioned like those of a Greek Chorus. As the screenplay developed the protagonists became more sharply drawn; the heroine became an Irish-American (to polarize the East/West dynamic further), but the original five-minute sequence remained as the basis of a climactic argument between the two lovers, two-thirds of the way through the story.

The journey from the five-minute film to its eventual form at one hundred minutes is represented in this book by the final screenplay and, as an addendum, the original five-minute script. This "final" screenplay is, of course, just the last version of a continuously evolving document. The final shooting script (what we had on paper just prior to the shoot) was longer; but in the cutting-room (and sometimes during the shoot itself) scenes were trimmed or eliminated, some sequences eventually unfolded in a different order, and there were one or two additions written at the very last minute. To avoid confusion, what appears here is the screenplay revised to match the finished film, and so, in that sense, it can be called "final."

To introduce the screenplay there is a letter from John Berger, who read several versions from one of its earliest incarnations through to its final (pre-shoot) form and with whom I shared many exhilarating conversations; together with an essay by Pankaj Mishra about the representation of Middle Eastern identity and its broader political and historical context.

Following the screenplay is a Q&A; an amalgamation of three such sessions recorded at the film's first festival screenings in Telluride, Toronto, and London, where I tried to find ways of answering a number of questions that were asked again and again. What motivated you to write this film? Why is it written in verse? Why does it end the way it does?

I began to write the film in the context of the precise global conditions of mid-September 2001, in an attempt to meet head-on the extreme difficulties we were all facing. Filmmaking, writing, all art, all forms of fiction seemed to have a question mark hanging over them. The notion of pure entertainment, or the story of an "inner voyage" divorced from the outer reality, seemed impossible, irrelevant, irresponsible. The challenge was how to contribute positively; how to help energize, clarify, connect, humanize. Fundamentally, how to be of use in such a state of emergency.

This entailed re-evaluating the whole business of being a filmmaker; my relationship with the image, with sound, and above all with language. To remain silent was impossible. But how to speak? Instinctively I turned to love and to verse. For love, ultimately, is a stronger force than hate; and verse—by virtue of its apparent artifice—paradoxically allows us to express the complexities of thought and experience in a distilled, natural way.

The process of making the film, the inventiveness necessitated by its low budget; the fine, committed ensemble cast; the dedicated producers and crew; all became indivisible from its content. This was no-waste, urgent filmmaking with all of us trying to go beyond our limits; dependent on each other's generosity and openness; working from a place of respect for each other's differences. At least a dozen different nationalities, from the East and West, worked in harmony together.

Perhaps *YES* is ultimately about the commonality beyond our cultural and political differences. It is also about the very small and the very large; from the micro-world of molecular science to the enormity of war; the giant clash of fundamentalisms, Eastern and Western. And in between those two worlds—somewhere on the middle of the scale of the very small to the very large—lies the human body with its desires, frailties, strengths, and ultimately, its mortality.

A Letter
by John Berger

Dear Sally,

At the time, storytellers never know exactly what they are telling. They are simply faithful to something they don't know. Later, after many tellings (or showings) in different circumstances with different listeners (or viewers), they begin to learn a bit more about the story that life gave them and they handed on. This is why I want to share with you now a few perceptions about the story which is now out there, which makes people weep or happy or furious, and which we so much talked about together—you and I—before it was really told.

YES. A film that irrefutably deserves its title. A film of affirmation. Which is *not* the same as a story with a happy ending.

Its storytelling, its narration, has chosen its own method. Again and again it proceeds through glances, hints, innuendos to arrive at a dénouement, a stripping away, a nakedness. The nakednesses, to which the narration leads, are every time surpris-

JOHN BERGER, novelist, essayist, playwright, art historian, and painter, is the author of art books including *Ways of Seeing*, a significant body of fiction including the Booker Prize-winner *G*, three screenplays, and four plays. Berger was born in London in 1926, and began his writing career at London's *New Statesman*. He now lives and works in a small village in the French Alps, which is explored in his fiction and nonfiction.

ing. (As they are in life, when the one looking is attentive. Dress renders us similar, nakedness renders each of us incomparable.)

The narration follows every character in this way—those in the background of the story and those up front. And this stitching-and-finally-unfurling narration comes from the events, substantial and imaginary, which make the story.

The story is presented by the cleaner who performs the role of a Greek chorus. (She, too, has her moment of nakedness.) The story is told by the glances and dance of the camera, which knows all and creates its own music and its own silences.

I see now that the story is about the way contradictions rhyme:

"You cannot look me in the face
And say I am your fall from grace."

The fact that all the people speak in verse confirms this rhyming in a way I hadn't foreseen. I knew the verse would allow people to speak out loud as if from their hearts—and would in this way, eliminate chatter. What I didn't foresee was how the verse would sharpen the knife-edge on which everything happens!

What do I mean by that? Why does the word "scimitar" keep coming back into my head as I write? It's a story about disappointments becoming affirmative. The other day I was looking again at your *Orlando* and there, too, no? Disappointments lead to poetry, let-downs inspire people to fly.

The places, the locations, are like characters, and the camera moves, all the while, around and in and through them with the same curiosity with which the cleaner examines and explains the house in which she's working. If the places in this story become characters, what is the *scene*? The arena of world politics today, nothing less, is the scene—and, above it, the sky to which everyone, at one moment or other, prays.

Desire, as shown in your film, is the offer—from one body to another—of a reprieve from the persistent pain of life. When the offer is accepted and reciprocated, the reprieve and its promise covers both parties for a while.

Wounds and desire—after a certain age—are inseparable. (Or perhaps at all ages? I suddenly remember being four!) The reprieve is a reminder of the grace—as distinct from the cruelty of nature. Isn't this why love poetry in all cultures refers so often to the beauties of nature?

Desire is as much to do with the taking away of the other's pain as with the mutual pursuit of pleasure. And the marvellous love scenes in *YES* recognise this.

This doesn't mean that desire is a narcotic or a painkiller. Rather, it is an alternative, shared use of physical energy and the special lucidity of the body, to bestow, if only for a brief moment, an exemption.

The body is everywhere in your film. A very unpuritan film—thus the absence of any need to idealise. What the film affirms is the longing of the body to become, to step (however small the steps) towards another state of being. In the insistence of such longings—not in their realisation or achievement—the eternal touches the human, and vice versa.

Every variety of desire—and there are so many—has its own metaphysic. In your film the metaphysic proposes that exemption is intimately connected with disappearance, and that disappearance equals immortality! This is what the final YES on the sand affirms.

With my love,

John

Introduction
by Pankaj Mishra

In the late 1960s, James Baldwin wrote an essay titled "To Be Baptized." It was a particularly bad time in that eventful decade. Martin Luther King Jr. and Malcolm X had just been assassinated; the Civil Rights movement still faced virulent opposition; and the Vietnam War had grown bloodier and appeared unwinnable. Baldwin blamed the great violence and confusion around him on Western nations, which he claimed

> have been caught in a lie, the lie of their pretended humanism; this means that their history has no moral justification, and that the West has no moral authority.... This lie, given the history and power of the Western nations, [has] become a global problem, menacing the lives of millions.

This sounds bitter. But then Baldwin was the son of a Harlem preacher, born poor and black in a white and racist country. Few white people in the West knew or cared much about a history that

PANKAJ MISHRA is the author of *The Romantics*, winner of the *Los Angeles Times's* Art Seidenbaum Award for First Fiction, and *An End to Suffering: The Buddha in the World*. He frequently contributes political and literary essays to *The New York Review of Books*, *Granta*, and the *Times Literary Supplement*. He was born in North India in 1969 and now lives in London and India.

had shaped relations between them and the rest of the world. But, perhaps, Baldwin could not avoid the knowledge that the brutal conquest and exploitation of peoples across the globe had helped create the edifice of modern Western civilization; that the building of this edifice had led to the uprooting and destruction of millions of native peoples across the world.

These insights embittered not only Baldwin but also many famous and obscure men of his generation. In our own politically more constricted and bourgeois times, such awareness about the nature of Western power appears too radical. It is rarely expressed in books and films produced in the West. Nevertheless, it creeps up on, and blights, the lives of many Asians and Africans who, fleeing the chaos of their postcolonial societies, have found refuge in the West.

It leads to bitterness and resentment, or what is described today as the "rage of the Muslim world." A historical understanding of how and when these passions arose may go some way in defusing them. But such understanding is not easily achieved by most people as they live in full, if unselfconscious, possession of the luxuries and privileges of the Western world.

Stereotypes, which a complaisant and frighteningly ignorant television and film industry is eager to provide, help avoid an examination of the vexed historical relationship between the West and the Muslim world. For some time now, long-bearded fanatics have signified the Arab's religion in the public realm; images of burka-clad women have explained his interpersonal relations; concepts such as "terrorism," "fundamentalism," and "Islamic totalitarianism" have summed up his complex past and present. Since 9/11, his fears, desires, and resentments have been mostly seen in the context of his apparent desire to pursue jihad against the infidels.

In this climate, the liberal view—that the Arab is simply a human being like you and me—seems salutary. But it often obscures the long and humiliating history of Western involvement in the Middle East, the greed for oil and territory, the hastily improvised puppet regimes, the CIA-organised coups against legitimate governments, all of which shape the Arab's self-perception more fundamentally than it does of anyone in the modern and prosperous societies of the West.

In Sally Potter's extraordinarily timely and perceptive film *Yes*, the very intelligent lead character, an Irish-American woman, knows little in the beginning of the complex humanity of the Lebanese man whom she, escaping a loveless marriage, falls into bed with. A lapsed Catholic, she is a dedicated research biologist, a firm believer in science and reason. But all her profound knowledge of the origins of life has not equipped her to cope with the little narcissisms of her philandering husband and teenage goddaughter, and, as it turns out, it cannot help her understand who her lover is and why he is in the West.

She discovers only gradually that he is a trained surgeon, whom the civil war in Lebanon has reduced to cutting vegetables in a restaurant kitchen in London, exposed to the taunts of his colleagues—damaged white men, who, adrift in the underworld of their affluent and uncaring society, take out their frustration on other unprotected minorities. ("This country's full of wankers dressed in sheets; asylum fucking seekers in our streets and taking all our fucking jobs...then what do they do? To give us thanks, they fucking blow us up!")

Seen through Potter's eye the Western landscapes through which her characters drift—tunnels, subway carriages, laboratories, car parks, hospitals—take on a desolate quality. But then this sterile West of concrete and artificial light is what lonely immigrants from less fragmented and alienated societies largely know. Potter also gives the Lebanese character an articulate self-aware-ness—angry, bitter, and tender—that is rarely found in portrayals of non-westerners, especially Arabs, in contemporary cinema.

He has a keen sense of the unfair world that the modern West has made after two hundred years of profit-driven political and economic systems that smashed older societies and forced their inhabitants into new ways. "From Elvis to Eminem, Warhol's art, I know your stories, know your songs by heart. But do you know mine?" He can not only feel but also express the pain and pathos of his diminishment in an alien country. "In your land," he tells his American lover, "I am not seen. I am…un-manned…You can't imagine with the white-skinned sense of privilege and human rights you take for granted, how I fight for every little thing."

Involved in a near-physical brawl with his racist colleagues, he is sacked from his job. His freshly wounded pride turns into polit-ical rage, which he vents on his white lover. "I have remembered who I am," he tells her, and goes on to list the sins of the West. ("The stupid things that you believe….You're "free"; but must defend that with a gun, a tank, a helicopter or a bomb….You think you know it all, that you're the best. One life of yours worth more than all the rest….You want our land, you want our oil…. You call that civilised?")

His Irish-American lover is bewildered. She had not expected this turn to their relationship. In any case, why should he hold her personally responsible for the greed and violence of the world she was born in?

Their private erotic world seems at an end. But then it was always likely to be broken into by larger events, subject as it was, like everything else, to what Wallace Stevens once called the "pressure of reality": "life in a state of violence, not physically

violent, as yet, for us in America, but physically violent for millions of our friends and for still more millions of our enemies and
spiritually violent, it may be said, for everyone alive."

Throughout the film, Potter uses the usually obscure figure of
the house-cleaner to remind us of this karmic truth of our inter-
connected world: of the cleanliness and purity that is an "illusion"
and the dirt that is shuffled around but "is always there." To
arrive at such knowledge is to begin to learn humility, to know
that, as the cleaner puts it, "everything you do or say is there, for-
ever" and to understand the importance of individual acts of kind-
ness and love.

In the last swift scenes of the film, the scientist returns to
Belfast to see her long-ailing communist aunt who dies convinced
of the futility of "a life spent longing for things you don't need."
The Lebanese returns to a baptism in Beirut. From these small
but symbolically momentous events—the end and the beginning
of life—they travel to reconciliation in Cuba. Here, in scenes full
of the glorious light and colours of the Caribbean, Potter brings
them together, believing that, as the poet said, "What will survive
of us is love."

Still, what is one to make of these journeys across a torment-
ed world? What does the affirmative "Yes," uttered in face of violence and suffering, mean? Perhaps, James Baldwin, an exile,
looking for love wherever he could, answered these questions
when he wrote:

What a journey this life is! Dependent, entirely, on
things unseen. If your lover lives in Hong Kong and cannot get to Chicago, it will be necessary for you to go to
Hong Kong. Perhaps, you will spend your life there, and
never see Chicago again. And you will, I assure you, as

long as space and time divide you from anyone you love, discover a great deal about shipping routes, air lanes, earthquakes, famine, disease, and war....And love will simply have no choice but to go into battle with space and time and, furthermore, to win....This is why one must say Yes to life and embrace it wherever it is found—and it is found in terrible places; nevertheless, there it is.

YES

A FILM BY
SALLY POTTER

final screenplay
24.09.04

The Screenplay

YES is set in the present in London, Belfast, Beirut and Havana.

The Characters

SHE:
: An American scientist of Northern-Irish descent (born and raised in Belfast), married to Anthony and living with him in London.

HE:
: A Middle-Eastern man, originally from Beirut where he worked as a doctor, now living in exile in London, and earning a living as a cook.

ANTHONY:
: A disillusioned English politician, once an idealist, married to SHE.

GRACE:
: The teenage goddaughter of Anthony and SHE.

KATE:
: Grace's mother, an old friend of SHE.

CLEANER:
: Works for Anthony and SHE.

VIRGIL:
: An Afro-Caribbean kitchen-worker.

BILLY:
: A Scottish kitchen-worker.

WHIZZER:
: An English washer-up.

AUNT:
: An Irish communist and atheist, now living in a nursing home in Belfast.

Note: The screenplay which follows has been edited and amended (following its evolution through the shoot and the rigours of the cutting room) to match its final form on the screen.

Front Titles

Microscopic images of the smallest visible particles of matter dance and float across the screen. They are as abstract and indecipherable as drawings, but undeniably alive.

The particles become dots and lines, electronic lines...that become...cells. These are quivering cells that float, randomly and catch the light...not cells, now, but grains—tiny grains of dust—drifting and sparkling in a beam of sunlight.

The dust is being shaken vigorously out of a sheet.

House / Bedroom – Day

The cleaner, the woman whose hands had shaken out the sheet, turns and speaks confidingly to the camera as she continues to make the bed in an immaculate white bedroom.

> *Cleaner:* They say my cleaning is the best
> *(to camera)* They've ever known. But cleanliness of course
> Is an illusion. Those of us who clean
> As a profession know the deeper source
> Of dirt is always there. You can't get rid
> Of it. You cannot hide or put a lid
> On it, as long as human life is there.
> It's us. The skin we shed, and then the hair....

We hear footsteps—angry footsteps—as someone comes up the stairs.

The cleaner picks up a hair from the bed and gingerly examines it as a woman (SHE) rushes angrily through the bedroom, and slams the door. The cleaner comes closer to the camera and whispers.

> *Cleaner:* I think of what I do as therapy
> *(to camera)* For homes. You know I often see the pain
> Imprinted on a bed. You spot a stain
> That should not be in there; of course you know

At once what's going on. But then you go
Into another room, the one he keeps
His papers in, or so he says...he sleeps
In there from time to time as well....

House / Study – Day

A door opens, briefly, onto a small, bare room. The room has a desk, with some files neatly stacked on it, and a single bed. Anthony is sitting, despairingly, on the edge of the bed, his head in his hands. Some music is playing, very loud; a guitar solo, the blues.

The cleaner, carrying a huge bundle of sheets, closes the door quietly and looks knowingly into the camera.

House / Staircase – Day

The cleaner dumps the sheets into a laundry basket and starts to climb the stairs; then hesitates and turns back to the camera.

> *Cleaner:*   What was I saying? Yes. It all relates.
> *(to camera)*   The evidence on things like dirty plates
>   And socks and underwear and other things
>   I shouldn't mention....

House / Lavatory – Day

She appears in the lavatory, bends over and stares into the pan.

> *Cleaner:*   ...that he sometimes flings
>   Into the toilet and thinks I won't see—
>   Ah—because he flushes, but unfortunately
>   He doesn't check it's gone. It's down to me
>   To try again—sometimes I fish it out....

She lowers her hand into the pan, gingerly removes a used condom and throws it into a pedal-bin.

Cleaner:	It's quicker in the end; it floats. I doubt
	They'll ever realise I know it all.
	They think that those of us who clean are small
	Somehow, in body and in mind; we fall
	Out of their line of sight; invisible,
	We work our magic. Indivisible
	One from the other; we're a mass, no soul,
	No rights to speak of, just a basic role
	To play in keeping their lives looking good.
	Cosmetic artists. That is what we should
	Be called. Or...dirt consultants.

Limousine – Night

SHE and her husband, Anthony, are sitting as far apart as possible in the back seat of a large, shiny limousine, each staring out of the window. The atmosphere between them is taut with tension. We hear her chaotic overlapping thoughts.

SHE:	*Nobody warned me, nobody said**
	That losing love is like being dead...
	Or deaf and dumb and blind and strangled....
	How could you? In our house?

She turns to her husband, angrily.

SHE:	How could you? In our house?
Anthony:	Oh, don't.
SHE:	Don't what?
Anthony:	Don't make a scene. Don't make it worse.

---

* Whenever dialogue appears in italics it indicates the character's "inner voice," or thoughts. We hear the words but do not see them spoken.

SHE: I'm not.

She turns and stares out of the window once more.

SHE: *Where? Our bed? The sofa? Or perhaps a chair?*

Embassy / Staircase & Entrance Hall (CCTV) – Night

A CCTV camera records SHE and Anthony as they mount a staircase in a large ornate building surrounded by other guests in evening dress. Anthony hands his coat automatically to a uniformed woman in the entrance hall without acknowledging her presence.

Embassy / Banquet Hall – Night

SHE is now standing conspicuously alone in a huge banquet hall, isolated from the other guests. She glances into a crowded ante-room where Anthony is standing with his hand resting on the back of a young woman, just a little too long for comfort.

A tall, dark man, HE, dressed in a tuxedo, walks out from the stark neon-lit kitchens into the candle-lit banquet hall. HE is heading for the long table laid for dinner, but then pauses, his attention caught by this elegant woman standing alone. HE stares at her for a moment and then approaches her cautiously.

HE: Forgive my question, but are you alright?

SHE: I'm fine, thank you.

HE: Are you sure?

SHE: Yes, quite.

HE: A woman left alone...if it was me...
       I wouldn't—

SHE: —wouldn't what?

4

HE: Let such a beauty
Out of my sight. Not for one moment. No.

Some time has passed and SHE is now sitting at the long banquet table opposite Anthony and is listening, abstractedly, to an older man as he talks to her; but her attention is really focussed on Anthony, who is flirting with the young woman seated next to him.

Meanwhile HE is serving wine and food with mock seriousness to guests at the table. HE is performing—clowning, without the other guests noticing—for her benefit. Eventually he manages to make her laugh.

Embassy / Washroom – Night

SHE has retreated to the washroom. She stares at herself in the mirror as she recalls her conversation with the stranger.

SHE: *A woman left alone...if it was me...*
I wouldn't—wouldn't what?
Let such a beauty
Out of my sight. Not for one moment. No.

And then she paces up and down as she recalls the conversation that followed.

HE: *And let me add: I'd like to steal*
(v.o.) *You from the man who cannot see*
That you're a queen. When are you free?

SHE: *My God, you're fast.*

HE: *Oh no, quite slow.*
(v.o.)

She stares at herself in the mirror again, smoothing down her dress.

SHE: *I don't believe this.*
I must say no, definitely.

Embassy / Staircase & Entrance Hall (CCTV) – Night

The jerky CCTV camera image reveals HE and SHE in the entrance hall, moving around each other like birds in a courtship dance. She hesitates, momentarily, then reaches into her bag, pulls out a business card and hands it decisively to him.

Embassy / Kitchen – Night

HE is chopping vegetables, whistling, looking pleased with himself. A telephone rings.

Taxi (New York) – Day

SHE is speaking from her mobile phone in a tunnel somewhere in New York City.

> SHE: It's you!
>
> HE: You knew.
> (v.o.)
>
> SHE: I guessed.
>
> HE: That's good.
> (v.o.) I said I'd call.
>
> SHE: I thought you would.

Alley Outside Embassy – Night

HE is standing, wearing a cook's uniform, in an alleyway outside the kitchens where he works, speaking into a mobile phone.

> HE: You're over there.

SHE: Quite far away—
(v.o.)

HE: You sound so near. And when are you—

Taxi (New York) – Day

SHE: —returning? In a day, or two.

HE: I'd like to meet.
(v.o.)

SHE: Yes, where? You say...

HE: Let's walk, somewhere, and eat.
(v.o.)

She smiles to herself before responding.

SHE: And talk.

A siren sounds in the background, and the sound of a car door slamming shut.

HE: What's that?
(v.o.)

SHE: My cab. I'm getting out.

HE: I cannot hear—
(v.o.)

SHE: —we'll have to shout!

HE: I'll call again....
(v.o.,
shouting)

SHE: Oh, good, yes, do!
(shouting)

HE: (v.o.)   I'm glad I found you....

The line disconnects.

Plaza (New York) – Day

SHE crosses a plaza, walking towards an enormous glass building. A skateboarder flies past her as she heads purposefully towards her destination, smiling to herself.

Conference Room (New York) – Day

And now SHE is standing at the head of a huge shiny table in a conference room high above the city. She looks out, confidently, at the group waiting attentively around the table.

> *SHE:*   I understand that you've invited me
> To make a case that life begins at three
> Hours; or at one, or two, or maybe four,
> As if there is a moment when we can be sure
> That we are human. You'll want evidence.
> Material. Not big ideas, nor common sense,
> But what is measurable, what you can see.
> And not just once, but many times, repeatedly.
> For this is science and that's what we do.

She pauses and looks around.

> *SHE:*   But wait a minute. Is this really true?
> *(cont'd)*   Could "objectivity" be just a point of view?
> We interpret what we see; and can see
> What we expect, in embryology.
> When a man first saw a sperm magnified
> He thought he saw a little man inside;
> And those that looked were sure that they could see
> One too; so eager were they to agree.
> Look at this. Man?

A slide appears on a screen. Some cells, clustering in a primitive embryological shape. And then a second...a similar image.

> SHE: Or mouse? The mystery
> *(cont'd) (o.s.)* Is that each cell knows its destiny....

House / Kitchen – Day

The cells become indistinct trembling shapes, which then come into focus as water gushing into a plughole.

It is the point of view of the cleaner who is scrubbing out a sink in an immaculate kitchen whilst Anthony eats breakfast and reads the newspaper. The telephone rings.

> Anthony: Yes? Who? Oh, Sister Maud, of course, hello.
> It's been a while. It has. How time does go....
> No, she's not here....Of course, I'll tell her, yes.
> I'm sure she meant to call....Oh I would guess
> The weekend, but of course one never knows....
> Yes, always working, that's the way it goes.
> And how is her aunt? Oh. Oh dear. How sad.
> Is it serious?

He is still reading the paper absentmindedly whilst the caller talks. And then his expression changes.

> Anthony: Oh dear....
> *(cont'd)*

His tone has changed. He looks sombre and chastened.

> Anthony: That does sound bad.
> *(cont'd)* Oh quite....Of course...I'll speak to her tonight.

The cleaner walks to the camera and whispers, confidingly, as Anthony scribbles a message in the background.

Cleaner: Except when she gets back he will be out.
(to camera)   That's how they organise their lives. I doubt
If they will see each other for a week.
They leave each other notes but rarely speak.

Anthony throws down the pen next to the message pad.

House / Hallway – Day

SHE throws down her keys onto a table in the hallway and starts picking up a pile of notes left for her by the telephone. She is about to read them when her mobile phone rings. She smiles when she realises who is calling her.

SHE: Hello!

Park – Day

It is spring, and SHE and HE are strolling through a London park. The trees are full of blossom, the ground covered in spring flowers. There is a something studiedly formal in the measured physical distance between them as they walk and talk, as if they are keeping something under control.

HE: Where are you from?

SHE: I'm Irish. From Belfast.

HE: You sound—

SHE: I know. American.
They took me there when I was ten.
And you?

HE: I'm from Beirut.

HE imitates the sound of guns firing, bombs exploding. They both laugh.

HE: My land is made of stones...
(cont'd)

HE gestures at the blossom on the trees around them.

HE: ...but we have trees
(cont'd) That blossom in the spring and then release
Their fruit. We have cherries, plums and peaches
And the queen of all, the tree that reaches
For the sun to fill its seed with gold:
The yellow fruit, the apricot. The old
And wisest say this fruit will keep them young....

HE leans towards her.

HE: And you can taste her secret with your tongue.
(cont'd)

Their eyes meet, briefly, and then she turns away.

SHE: Potato is our apricot. We bake
We boil, we mash, we fry; and then we make
A flour of it for dumplings in our stew
Or bread or scones or pancakes....
The famine haunts us still, you see.

HE: We too are haunted by our dead, it seems.
They speak to us in riddles in our dreams;
So many killed. They ask the question—why?
Did we have to die?

SHE: Look...shall we think of something sad?
(ruefully) This conversation's far too light.

HE: That's bad....
Yes. Absolutely. You are right.

*They smile at each other, fleetingly. And then she touches him lightly,
consolingly, on the arm.*

SHE: My auntie in Belfast once said to me
Survivors can't forget; the memory
Is all that's left. We cannot let it go.
If it is lost, then who will ever know?
She brought me up. I loved her so.

HE and SHE are walking once again and SHE is talking volubly as HE listens attentively. It seems she has not really been listened to in this way for a long time; the words have been released and are flowing out of her.

SHE: My parents went away when I was two.
(cont'd)   They said they'd fetch me in a month, but then
A month became a year...my father flew
Back home from time to time. I never knew
When I would go. Do you believe in God?

HE is about to answer, but she continues, rapidly, her speech barely able to keep up with her thoughts.

SHE: She didn't; so I had to pray
(cont'd)   At school, then go back home and say
I thought that reason was the way,
The light, and that God was dead....

Streets – Day

HE is leading SHE down an alleyway between two crumbling mansion blocks, carefully helping her to avoid the broken paving stones, as she talks, on and on. It seems as if neither of them is really concentrating on what she is saying anymore.

SHE: This was a Catholic school; they fed
Us catechism, fear of hell,
And fear of punishment as well.
They hit us hard to do us good
And told us that we never would
Survive without our faith. My aunt
Said they were hypocrites. You can't

Imagine how it was to be alone
With such a split: but to atone
For sinful doubt I searched for truth,
With all the passion of my youth.

HE gestures towards a doorway, breathing heavily.

Apartment / Hallway – Day

HE and SHE are now standing in the small entrance hall just inside the front door of his apartment. HE is undoing the buttons on her coat, one by one.

>   *HE:*   You found it?

>   *SHE:*   Science.

HE looks at her, questioningly, for a moment.

>   *HE:*   So you think that you
>   Can penetrate the mind of God.

>   *SHE:*   I do...
>   Not know...if God has a mind. Or if there
>   Is a God. I don't...know....

They are standing very close to each other. HE touches her hair, lightly.

>   *HE:*   Such golden hair....
>   *(murmuring)*   We can agree—

>   *SHE:*   —to disagree? How true.
>   *(murmuring)*   I'm talking far too much. Now, what of you?

HE begins to sing, softly, in Arabic, into her ear. She listens, transfixed.

>   *HE:*   We'd rather sing than speak. It leaves us free...
>   *(softly)* To mourn, or to rejoice. Ultimately
>   There always is a choice.

They gaze at each other. She starts to unbutton his overcoat.

> SHE: Ah, so, you see....
> *(murmuring)* We're not so different, really, you and me.

They start to remove each others' clothes one by one, gradually falling into each others' arms.

Apartment / Bedroom – Day

SHE opens her eyes and turns slowly towards HE who is lying beside her. HE gazes wonderingly at her. She becomes shy under such intense scrutiny.

> SHE: Speak to me.

> HE: Of what? What is there to say?

> SHE: Too much...or nothing...please try, anyway.

HE thinks for a moment, and then:

> HE: Well, I adore...the number one.
> One you, one me, one moon, one sun.

> SHE: Must I revolve around you then? Am I
> *(playfully)* The silver planet circling round the gold?
> Are you the source of light and heat, whilst I
> Am shadow, pulling watery tides, and cold?

> HE: You hear a meaning where there's none, I fear—
> I spoke of one. A number. An idea.
> My preference for...

HE grins.

> HE: ...the single state, that's all.
> *(cont'd)*

SHE: Single is a word based on illusion.
Life itself develops from a fusion.
Two is joining, letting go, attraction
And rejection, yes and no....
It's not a solo but a sweet duet
That's played to bring us here, and then forget
How it was before we met the other.
It was two that brought us to the mother....

She stares into the distance for a moment.

SHE: *And desire that led us to the lover.*

HE: You're right. But now I'd like to speak of three.
(*lightly*) Admit: there's you and him, and now there's me.

SHE: Oh God...let's hide inside the number four.
A house with walls; and with a door
That closes onto chaos—

HE: —we've gone too far. I forgot.
The thought that precedes one, the thought that's not;
The void, the vast and endless state of none;
Containing, holding, god-like; it's the one
And only number that we really need.
Nought is the majesty
That rules our lives, unseen, and silently.

She sits up and gazes into the distance, thoughtfully.

SHE: Nice. But...a bit too mystical for me.
Someone invented zero so that we
Could count and measure the unthinkably
Large unwieldy numbers. And it was then—
By multiplying to the power of ten—
That we began to measure space, and so
To time....

HE smiles at her as she pauses, briefly.

> SHE: You tricked me!
> *(cont'd)*

> HE: No!

> SHE: Yes. You did. Of course.
> You start with one, then give yourself the source
> Of all the numbers.

> HE: No, lovely lady. All I meant to say
> *(softly)* Was this: you are the one. The light of day,
> The velvet night, the single rose, the hand
> I want to hold, the secret country, land
> Of all my longings. There. You have my word.

Laboratory – Day

SHE is sitting in her laboratory in front of a microscope, lost in reverie, smiling happily to herself. Eventually she sighs and brings her attention back to her work.

Embassy / Kitchen – Day

HE is humming to himself contentedly as he stands skillfully chopping vegetables.

Three kitchen hands—Virgil (Afro-Caribbean), Billy (Scottish) and Whizzer (English)—are working nearby, piling dishes into a dishwasher and scrubbing pans in the enormous sinks in the hot and steamy atmosphere. Virgil is watching HE knowingly.

> Virgil: I used to lay the blondes who came my way.
> And they were ready for it, night or day.
> I'd look at them—I wouldn't say a word—
> And they were on their backs, as if they'd heard
> A heavenly command. And then they'd cry.

At first with pleasure, like they'd never had.
And then they'd phone you up and drive you mad.
The weeping and the wailing, and the rest.
They'd ruin it! At first they were the best;
Those babes...but now at last I've seen the light.

Billy and Whizzer look at each other and groan. HE smiles to himself.
Virgil continues, oblivious.

Virgil:	Temptation's there to teach us how to fight.
(cont'd)	The devil comes in every shape and size;
	Those that resist him get the prize.
	The prize is Jesus, thank the Lord above;
	He is the maximum top source of love!

Billy stops loading dishes for a moment.

Billy:	Now hold it there. Some girls may be tarts,
	But they're not evil; they've got broken hearts.
	They do it 'cause it's all they know. They're used
	For sex when they are kiddies. They're abused
	From start to finish, then they're on the streets
	And taking drugs instead of eating sweets.
	They haven't got a chance. Back home I'd walk
	Around a bit and chat with them, sometimes; just talk....

Whizzer snorts derisively.

Whizzer:	You'd what? Just talk? You're not that fucking good.
	You'd fucking do it if you fucking could.
Billy:	You know fuck all about my fucking life.
(angrily)	
Whizzer:	I know you're fucking skint. So did your wife.
Billy:	You fucking leave that out of fucking this.
Whizzer:	I'm only joking. Can't I take the piss?

Virgil has been smiling to himself throughout this exchange.

    Virgil: The difference is I never had to pay.

    Whizzer: Yes, so you fucking always fucking say.
                No fucking woman's free of charge. No way.
                You fancy one, but there's no fucking lay—

    Billy: —unless you buy the drinks all fucking night.
  (muttering)

    Virgil: It's not the drinks. You have to treat them right.
              They want respect—

    Whizzer: —respect?

    Virgil: And dignity.

    Whizzer: Oh Jesus Christ, I've seen the fucking light.
                You shag them, then chuck them away,
                And now you've got the fucking cheek to say
                That you respect them. And they're fucking white.
                And fucking blonde—

    Billy: —oh, come on now, big boy;
  (placatingly) You'll pull a girlie soon. Don't start a fight.

    HE: I saw a woman once, upon a bus.
  (quietly)

The others turn at the sound of his voice, surprised. It would seem that HE doesn't often participate in their conversations.

    HE: She was a foreigner; not one of us.
  (cont'd) She sat alone, this tourist from the west;
             Her trembling bosom in a skin-tight vest.
             The men were staring at her from behind,
             The same scenario in every mind.
             There was a television—

Whizzer:	—on the bus?
	With fucking videos and all, like us?
Billy:	Don't interrupt. What happened next? Poor lass...
Whizzer:	Each fucking Arab got a piece of ass!
HE:	An image came up on the shaking screen.
Whizzer:	A porno movie! Fucking gang-bang scene!
Billy:	Shut up!
HE:	He's right—the image was obscene.
	But not the way you think. It was a girl—
	A young one, fair and fresh—a lovely pearl,
	With long fair hair that blew around her head
	Like golden candy floss, as she shot dead
	One man after another with her gun.
	We stared, and sweated, as the blazing sun
	Beat down upon the bus, but didn't care.
	She wore a costume that was hardly there....

Whizzer has stopped moving and is staring open-mouthed at HE who continues to work, dexterously, as he speaks.

HE:	A little piece of fabric round her hips
(cont'd)	And covering her breasts; and on her lips
	Some glossy red. And every time she killed
	A man her lips would open. Yes, she spilled
	Their blood with pleasure. And she wore a flag.
	The cloth that covered her was not a rag,
	It was a symbol: stars and stripes. I swear,
	This was a blonde American. They share
	Their women's bodies with the world, you see.

Virgil nods, knowingly.

Virgil:	It's true. They have no shame or modesty.

Billy:	Come on now, lads, it's not all black and white.
	They may be wrong, but you're not in the right.

Billy gestures at HE.

Billy:	Where he comes from the lasses wear the veil.
(cont'd)	They've got no life, it's like they're in a jail.

Whizzer:	Too fucking right! Some wear those things like beaks.
	They look like fucking crows, give me the creeps....

Billy:	Aye, they're oppressed....

Whizzer:	But what about the vest?
	That one up front, all trembling and the rest?

HE smiles, wickedly, and then:

HE:	She was a foreigner, therefore a guest,
	And we were hosts, therefore we were polite.

Whizzer:	That's all that happened? What a load of shite.
(disappointed)	

HE smiles to himself.

School – Day

SHE is standing by her car watching her teenage goddaughter, Grace, as she saunters out of the school gates, surrounded by a multi-racial group of friends, all dressed in shapeless school uniforms, some of them wearing traditional headscarves. They are laughing and talking raucously, their energy spilling in all directions.

SHE is glowing, lost in her private reverie, as she gazes at the girls.

Grace sees her godmother and races over and kisses her on the cheek.

> SHE: Hi, gorgeous!

Car – Day

As they drive off together, Grace pulls down the passenger mirror and gazes at herself, critically.

> Grace: I'm feeling fat. What do you think?

> SHE: Oh darling girl, you're lovely, and you're more....

Swimming Pool / Changing Rooms – Day

SHE and Grace are in the changing rooms of a swimming pool, standing side by side in front of a long mirror. SHE is wearing a sensible swimsuit and Grace is wearing a snazzy bikini and sarong. The focus of attention is Grace as she makes herself up, but now and then SHE glances at herself, appraisingly, as if seeing herself through a stranger's eyes.

> SHE: You'll have a stream of lovers who'll adore
> You; not just for your eyes and glossy hair
> And for your slender body—don't despair—
> You are not fat. But even if you were
> You'd still be beautiful—

> Grace: —you see! You think
> I'm huge! I knew it!—

> SHE: —I did not infer
> That you were over-large in any way.

SHE turns sideways to look at herself, lifting her chest slightly, pulling her stomach in. Grace has stopped making herself up and is studying her godmother curiously.

> SHE: What your godmother is trying to say
> (cont'd) Is this; Grace, there is so much more to you

Than your reflection. So much more to do
Than stand and stare, obsessed with...

SHE strokes herself dreamily for a moment, and then turns back to Grace, who has been watching her closely.

> SHE: You are not fat!
> (cont'd) Don't waste another breath of yours on that!

> Grace: But don't you worry about you?
>   The lines and stuff?

SHE looks at Grace and then turns back to the mirror, and touches her face, lightly, questioningly, with her fingertips.

SHE and Grace walk past some showers where a cleaner is mopping the floor.

> Grace: Pursuit of beauty is the rule;
> (cont'd) They say you mustn't let it go
>   Without a struggle. I'll be there
>   With colour covering every hair
>   That's grey, and cutting straight away
>   If there's a wrinkle. You wait and see.
>   I'll do it when I'm twenty-three.

They disappear around a corner. The cleaner stops mopping and turns to look into the camera.

Swimming Pool – Day

SHE is swimming through the turquoise water of the pool.

Eventually she hauls herself out of the water and sits down next to Grace, who is reclining on a lounger.

> SHE: How's school?

> Grace: Okay.

Silence.

> SHE: What interests you most?

> Grace: You mean: what's fun?

> SHE: I know you like to boast
> That you're a party girl without a brain.
> I don't believe you, Grace. Now, try again.

Grace shrugs.

> Grace: If you insist, I suppose there's something I
> Quite like to think about. I find I lie
> In bed and then I start to drift and dream.
> Things really aren't as they seem....

Grace breaks off for a moment to gaze into the distance with a troubled expression. SHE stares at her profile, imagining what Grace is about to say.

> SHE: That's true enough. Look closer and we see
> That everything is really chemistry.
> The world is made of sulphur and of tin,
> Of phosphorous and lead and nitrogen...

SHE closes her eyes and drifts into reverie.

> SHE: *Of mercury, of zinc and hydrogen,*
> (cont'd) *Of gold and silver and uranium,*
> *Of carbon, iron and vanadium,*
> *Argon, potassium, titanium....*

Grace's attention has also turned inward. She puts on some dark glasses and stares moodily into space.

SHE opens her eyes and turns back to Grace.

> SHE: So, Grace, what do you really want to be?
> (cont'd)

Grace: Famous.

Apartment – Day

SHE is lying in bed in her lover's small, modest apartment. From the look
of the bed, and her flushed face, it seems that they have been making love.
She is laughing as HE whistles whilst making her a post-lovemaking snack
in the kitchen.

HE pauses for a moment, a knife in his hand, and looks at her. Something
in her open expression compels him to begin to speak.

> *HE:*   I was a doctor. With a knife.
> I cut the flesh to save the life.
> A surgeon. Yes. My father, too.
> But I came here. What could I do?
> I use my knife to cut the food.
> I do it well. I'm very good
> At cutting meat. I chop, I dice
> The ham—which I don't eat—I slice
> It wafer-thin, so delicate,
> Like lady's lace. It's very nice
> To look at; silky to the touch.
> I like my work, yes, very much.

> *SHE:*   But surely, truly, don't you feel
> You're wasting what you were? The task
> You trained for? Why did you choose
> To leave a country that could use
> Your talents properly?

HE lowers the plate and its lovely delicacy onto a small table.

> *HE:*   No reason. Why should I
> *(lightly ironic)*   Jump in a plane, and grieving, fly
> Half way around the world?
> Perhaps—yes! I forgot!

I was a surgeon! Now the plot
Has changed; the story's been revised....
The hero's been reduced, down-sized,
A lower kind of man. A cook!
The kind of man you wouldn't look
At—is that what you want to say?
Not good enough for you today?

SHE shakes her head in disbelief. HE stands silently and very still in the kitchen, holding his kitchen knife, looking down. HE hesitates, momentarily, and then continues.

> *HE:*
> *(cont'd, quietly)*
>
> One night I saved a man from certain death.
> I operated; when he took a breath
> I knew that he was safe and I felt good.
> I'd done my job, with skill, the way I should.
> I turned to go, but standing in the door
> Were three men that I knew, but I was sure
> They hadn't come to talk, for it was late,
> They carried guns, and in their eyes was...hate.
> They told me I was wasting precious skill
> And time on someone that might later kill
> A child of theirs, or mine. Before my eyes
> They shot him dead. They said: you can't disguise
> One of "them" as a patient. From now on
> You treat our people only, do you hear?
> I packed my bags at once, and I was gone.
> They'd killed a man and murdered an idea—
> That doctors answer to a human need
> Without a thought of colour, or of creed—
> And then had the effrontery to claim
> That they had done it in my people's name.
> It's something that you wouldn't understand.

> *SHE:*
> *(softly)*
>
> Oh but I do. You're not the only ones....
> *I feel your story in my blood and bones....*

She watches him as he moves about restlessly in the kitchen, preoccupied with his thoughts and feelings.

SHE:　I see a father, calling to his son
(cont'd)　I see the houses crumble, dust and stones.
　　　　I hear the gunfire, and the knock at night
　　　　Upon the door. I see the women's fright;
　　　　I hear the adolescent called to fight;
　　　　I see him march away in morning light
　　　　And not look back. He knows his mother
　　　　Weeps. She fears that she will lose another
　　　　Son. She's buried two already. Listen
　　　　To her litany as the tears glisten
　　　　On her cheeks, and to the bell that's ringing
　　　　Calling her to church, to join the singing
　　　　And to praise the Lord.

HE turns and looks at her from the kitchen, and sees her sorrowful expression.

SHE:　Yes, I know of so-called holy war.
(cont'd,　You do not have to go
quietly)　So very far from here to find it.

HE crosses the room with the food he has prepared and offers it to her, graciously, then kisses the back of her neck, tenderly.

Football Pitch – Day

Four hands grip some battered mesh fencing. The hands belong to SHE and her friend Kate, who are both dressed in running clothes, and are stretching on the edge of an inner-city football pitch. Kate is scrutinising SHE, curiously.

Kate:　You're looking good.

SHE:　Well, thank you, Kate....am I?

Kate:　I think I see a sparkle in your eye.

Kate looks questioningly at her. SHE bends over, to hide her face as she smiles to herself.

26

Kate:	But as for me...I'm tired. My limbs are sore,
(cont'd)	My feet are aching. Oh I'm such a bore,
	I'm sorry. I've just been at home and you
	Have gone half-way around the world.

They start to move off, jogging around the perimeter of the pitch.

Kate:	How you can climb
(cont'd)	Out of your bed at dawn when you've had three
	Or four hours sleep at most...but then you see
	That is the difference between you and me.
	I simply do not have your energy.

| *SHE:* | Oh, what nonsense. You're amazing. |
| | You have far more stamina than me. |

| *Kate:* | What was the conference about? |

SHE:	They want an easy ethical way out,
	So that the public doesn't have to feel
	We're killing living things—

| *Kate:* | —but are you? |

| *SHE:* | Kate! |

| *Kate:* | I'm sorry, but you know I really hate |
| | To think of those poor little— |

| *SHE:* | —cells. They're cells. That's all they are. |
| *(impatiently)* | |

| *Kate:* | Sorry! |

They run on in silence for a moment.

Kate:	Do they feel pain?
(cont'd,	
tentatively)	

SHE: *Why must I justify my work again?*

They stop running, each lost in their own thoughts. And then something in Kate's expression drives SHE to change the subject.

SHE: How are the children?

Kate: Fine. The little ones as usual are divine....
        But of course the giantess is trouble.
        She stays upstairs in the heap of rubble
        She calls her room and never talks to me.
        I hear you took her out the other day.
        How was it?

SHE: Lovely. For me, anyway.

Kate: Oh yes? But then she so looks up to you.
        She thinks I'm dull.
        Sometimes I wish that I could get away,
        Like you. Just take off on some sunny day....

They move off together again.

SHE: One airport's like another.
        I used to dream of travel, now
        I pack and unpack suits and shoes.
        Suits and shoes: that's all they see!
        The haircut and the clothes, even with me.
        I envy you.

Kate: Oh? Why?
(quickly)

SHE: Because you're free...
        To wear your ancient tracksuits all the time
        And t-shirts covered in your baby's slime—

Kate stops in her tracks.

28

Kate:	—well, thanks. That lovely portrait really gives
(angrily)	A feeling for the life a mother lives.
	A less important job, the one I do.
	Thank God our mothers did it, though, or you
	Would not be here at all and nor would I.

Silence as they avoid each others' gaze.

SHE:	*Why is it that we always end this way?*
	Competing for who suffers most?
	Perhaps you did it right: a single mum...
	My so-called "open marriage" has become...
	We just can't talk...so many lies....

| Kate: | Well, I guess that's what happens when love dies. |

SHE looks at Kate, startled.

SHE:	Kate, you know us both.
	You're his friend too and so I'm really loathe
	To say too much....What has he said to you?

| Kate: | Oh, nothing, really.... |

Kate smiles reassuringly at her and runs off.

SHE runs in pursuit of Kate. They continue jogging side by side into the distance.

Laboratory – Day

SHE puts a petri dish into a refrigerator, closes the door, pulls off her rubber gloves, dumps them in a rubbish bin, and walks determinedly out of the laboratory.

Restaurant – Afternoon

SHE and HE are sitting opposite each other at a table in a smart expensive-looking restaurant, at the end of a meal. They are whispering to each other as waiters clean up and other customers gradually vacate their tables.

HE: *(whispering)*	Oh lovely goddess, whore and tramp You are my love, you light the lamp That guides me through the velvet night Towards you.

SHE: *(whispering)*	Hold me. Hold me tight.

His hand has disappeared somewhere under the table, under her skirt.

HE:	Your voice, your paleness, your perfume, Your presence haunts me. In my room I wait for you, filled with desire. Your hungry look ignites my fire; Oh lady, what then can I do But burn? I am in flames for you.

SHE: *(breathlessly)*	Before I knew you, now I know I was not living. This is so Much more than anything I've felt.... Oh my love: you hold me and I melt. I am not solid anymore.... I am a feeling. Call me whore! I'll ask for more! The names you give Me—names I never would forgive If spoken to me in the street— Somehow, from you, my love, they're sweet....

They move apart, momentarily, as a waiter approaches the table and discreetly places the bill in front of HE. SHE pulls it automatically towards her, without looking at it.

The waiter looks knowingly at them both, winks at HE and walks away. HE looks slightly uncomfortable, but then turns his attention back to her, with an added edge to his voice.

His hand has disappeared under her skirt once more.

> HE: What can I give you, lady luck?
>   What other words and names? I'll fuck
>   You as a mistress, as a queen;
>   I'll worship you with words obscene
>   And ugly, all the more to show
>   How I adore you; bring you low
>   With language from the gutter;
>   Hear me now, I'll gently mutter
>   Things into your ear; flowing streams
>   Of words from fantasies and dreams
>   You've not confessed to anyone.

> SHE: Yes—please!
>   Yes—say it all!

She has pulled out her credit card and put it on the table next to the bill.

> HE: Let forbidden thoughts be heard—

> SHE: Yes!

> HE: Let the hidden parts be seen.

> SHE: Yes!

> HE: The only
>   Danger is that all the lonely
>   Private places you have been to
>   Might dissolve, and you'll be seen to
>   Blossom. Dancing, singing, humming,
>   Laughing...come here, love, you're coming.

She leans into him, ecstatically, trembling, hiding her face in his shoulder.
Then she sits back, laughing, as he licks his fingers and smiles.

House / Entrance– Afternoon

Anthony is standing reading a newspaper in the stark white drawing room whilst listening to his favourite blues, playing very loud as usual. The doorbell rings. He throws down the newspaper and crosses the room to look at the video entry-phone. It is Grace, standing waiting expectantly in her school uniform. He turns the music down, opens the door and smiles, a little too brightly.

> *Anthony:* Grace. Come in!
>
> *Grace:* Oh…is she here?
>
> *Anthony:* Not now.
> But come on in and wait, Grace, anyhow.

Grace steps into the hallway, tentatively, and then pulls her mobile phone out of her schoolbag and dials a number.

Restaurant – Afternoon

SHE and HE are still sitting at the restaurant table. She kisses him, passionately. Her mobile phone rings. She doesn't hear. Or doesn't care.

House / Drawing Room – Afternoon

Grace is still standing in the hallway outside the formal white drawing room, her mobile phone pressed to her ear. Eventually she snaps it shut, glances at Anthony, and shrugs.

Anthony stands watching her, a glass of whisky in his hand. There is a tense, awkward atmosphere as he tries, a little too hard, to be warm and relaxed with his goddaughter. He gestures towards the sofa.

> *Anthony:* Do make yourself at home. Come; sit by me.

Grace crosses the room and sits down at the far end of the sofa.

Anthony: *(cont'd)*	Something to drink? Perhaps you'd like some tea?
Grace:	No thanks.

Silence. Anthony sits down beside her on the sofa. She looks uneasy.

Anthony:	How's school?
Grace:	Fine. Not too much to say.
Anthony:	I see. Well, Grace, you don't give much away. You're very wise!
Grace:	I do my best.
Anthony:	But you don't have to do a thing.

Anthony smiles at Grace.

Anthony: *(cont'd)*	You just have to be. The rest comes later. When you're old, like me.
Grace: *(brightly)*	I'm not that young. And you're not that old.
Anthony:	You're sweet.

He reaches out and takes her hand. She looks at him warily with her big dark eyes.

Anthony: *(cont'd)*	Look, Grace...may I confide in you?

Grace looks embarrassed. She opens her mouth to speak but thinks better of it.

Anthony: *(cont'd)*	Your godmother and I...she thinks I'm...cold. But it's her, you see. I have feelings too....

The cleaner walks in holding a duster in her hand. She takes in the scene at a glance, looks into the camera, knowingly, and then withdraws discreetly.

Apartment – Afternoon

Feet are moving like knives, cutting through the air. HE, dressed in a singlet and trousers, is balancing on a small table, performing a rapid, joyful folk-dance for SHE, who lies in bed, watching him, entranced. As he turns, gesturing expressively, he hits the ceiling lamp, which starts to spin. She laughs and he laughs with her. HE continues to dance and SHE seems to be watching him, but her attention has gradually drifted inward. Her expression changes seamlessly from happiness to anxiety.

Shoe Shop – Day

Grace is trying on a pair of shoes; teetering, strappy high-heels. SHE watches as Grace gazes at herself in the mirror, posing, and posturing in the vivid pink lights as loud repetitive music pounds through the shop.

Grace:	He said you're cold.
SHE:	Who?
Grace:	Your husband, silly!
SHE:	Oh God.
	And what the hell was he—
Grace:	—I came to see you. You were out.
	And then he told me all about
	His secret feelings.
SHE:	Oh, I see.
	That must have been...exactly when?
Grace:	He held my hand as well.

SHE: Oh Jesus Christ. And then?

House / Drawing Room – Day

Grace is sitting on the sofa next to Anthony, as before. She looks uncomfortable.

Anthony: I need to talk at the end of my day.
            She feels I've compromised or lost my way,
            So she won't listen. She will never learn
            What changing things, in practice, has to be.

He gets up and starts to pace backwards and forwards.

Anthony: She's like a student. Her mentality
(cont'd) Is as it was when we first met; all dreams,
            And talk and grand ideas and lofty schemes
            About "society" and "truth." I try
            To do something to right the wrongs—yet I
            Somehow am now the enemy, whilst she
            Does science and retains integrity,
            Or so she thinks. She always has to feel
            That she's the underdog, the one that's real,
            While I am false, somehow. And English, too
            Of course, while she is Irish through and through....
            The fact is that she left when she was ten!
            She grew up in America. But then
            It suits her to forget that on the whole.
            She claims her roots and so can play the role
            Of the oppressed. Right—so tell me why
            She never seems to find the time to fly
            Back home to see one of the very last
            True communists—her auntie in Belfast?

He focuses on Grace for a moment who looks embarrassed by his long, angry monologue.

Apartment – Day

HE and SHE are lying fully dressed next to each other on top of the bed. HE has a remote control device in his hand and we hear heavy romantic music playing on the television.

Their body language indicates greater ease and familiarity with each other than before; but with the familiarity comes a casual self-absorption. While he stares at the television she is gazing, unseeing, into the middle-distance, talking on and on without noticing his reaction.

SHE: To say those things to her—he has abused
       Us both. She doesn't need to know how we
       Have organised our marriage...

HE looks at her sharply. She continues, oblivious.

SHE: ...and then he
(cont'd)   Said things about...she so looks up to me!
       I could kill him. I could shoot him dead.
       Our goddaughter! I can't believe he said...

HE: Have you ever seen a body full of bullets?

SHE: As a matter of fact—

HE: —you people—

SHE: —who?—

HE: —are so naive—

SHE: —what?—

HE: —the stupid things that you believe.
       You think there is no pain
       That cannot be forgotten, and no chain
       That fetters you that cannot be undone.

36

You're "free"; but must defend that with a gun,
A tank, a helicopter or a bomb....

SHE: So no-one thinks that way where you come from?
       Why suddenly accuse me in this way?

HE: I have a different point of view
       On life and death.

HE switches channels. The sound of explosions, carnage. She grabs the
remote control device and switches off the television.

SHE: But is that really true?

HE: You are a scientist, and from the West.
       You think you know it all, that you're the best.
       One life of yours worth more than all the rest.

She stares at him.

SHE: Hello? Is it me that you're talking to?
       What do you know about my point of view?
       And, come to that, about the work I do?

HE: You do not seem to work much, anyway.
(smilingly,   I work at night. But you...here...in the day....
ironically)

SHE: Jesus! What's going on? What did I say?
       It seems that you know nothing of my life.

HE: I know that you are married. You're a wife.
       A woman with a lover—in the day—
       Perhaps another one at night? Or two?

She stares at him and then reaches over to caress him.

SHE: I don't have lovers. There is only you.
(softly)

37

Embassy / Kitchen – Night

HE is at work in the noisy, steamy kitchens. HE looks troubled as he listens distractedly to the three kitchen workers, who are, as usual, in the middle of an animated conversation.

The kitchen is draped with tawdry Christmas decorations and the kitchen workers have wrapped bits of tinsel in their hair and overalls.

> *Virgil:* Oh shit, man, I was saved from worse than sin.
> My life was ugly. I ate out of bins,
> You know I sank that low? I had no pride.
> The dirt on me...and in my mouth....I lied
> With every breath. I didn't have a friend
> Left in the world...they gave up in the end.
> It was hopeless! And it was all because
> I turned away from Jesus. It was hell.
> But then He found me and He made me well
> Again! Oh praise the Lord, the Mighty One,
> Who gave this undeserving world His Son!

> *Whizzer:* You think it's you that fucking turned away?
> He saw your fucking face and thought: no way!

> *Billy:* Don't mock the man. But look, I can't believe
> In any father that would go and leave
> His son in such a mess. Why didn't He
> Come sooner? None of it makes sense to me.

> *Whizzer:* Too right it don't. You've got to fucking think.
> I'm God, you're dirt, I wash you in the sink
> Of holy fucking water. Well, what for?
> For one less sinner banging at the door
> Of heaven when it's all too fucking late?

> *Virgil:* The Lord is merciful—

Whizzer:	—Oh I fucking hate
	This crap. There ain't no God. It's fucking shite.
	Or if there is, he's full of fucking spite.

| Billy: | It's you that's negative. |

| Whizzer: | Don't pick on me! |

| Billy: | I'm not. But every cunt's your enemy. |

| Whizzer: | Too fucking right! If Jesus chose that fuck |
| | Instead of me, now who's got all the luck? |

Virgil:	His heart is big enough for you as well.
(calmly)	If you repent your sins you're saved from hell.
	He will forgive the things you've said today.
	Just go down on your knees and start to pray.

| Whizzer: | Fuck off! You fucking wanker! There's no way! |
| | That wasn't what I fucking meant to say. |

| HE: | What did you mean? |

Whizzer wheels round to look at HE.

| Whizzer: | You picking on me too? |

| HE: | I only asked. |

| Whizzer: | What do you fucking do? |
| | Go down the fucking mosque? Dark fucking horse. |

HE starts to parody this sinister description, twirling his moustache.

| HE: | Oh, infidel! |

| Whizzer: | Oh, what? Of fucking course! |
| | You're a fanatic. One of them. |

HE play-acts cutting his throat, smiling broadly at Whizzer.

Billy: Be careful, laddie.
(quietly)

HE: Why, are you afraid?
(suddenly
serious)

Billy: Don't be ridiculous.

Virgil: The lamb has strayed....

Whizzer: What fucking lamb?

Virgil: The lamb of God's in hell.
He was in Paradise, and then he fell.

Whizzer: I've had it with this fucking God and shit.
There ain't no paradise, this fucking crap is it.
This country's full of wankers dressed in sheets;
Asylum fucking seekers in our streets
And taking all our fucking jobs. Arab wanks!

Virgil: Easy, easy—

Billy is trying to placate Whizzer, to no avail.

Billy: Now, son—

Whizzer: And then what do they do to give us thanks?
They fucking blow us up!

HE: You've got it wrong.
(quietly)

Whizzer: That fucking jihad war, it won't be long!

HE: The war is fought inside the soul of man.

He struggles, doing everything he can
To overcome his base desires; the part
Of him that's animal and has no heart;
The self that's primitive and has no mind;
That's why there is a law. Islamic law's not kind
But it is fair.

Whizzer: A bomb's not fucking fair.
You Arab shites are evil, you don't care.

HE: To you we're all the same from "over there."
(shouting) You're ignorant!

Whizzer: Now don't you fucking dare—

HE: —You celebrate your ignorance with joy.
You should be studying. You're just a boy,
And living on the street.

Whizzer: So fucking what?

Whizzer throws the frying pan he was washing into the sink, suddenly apoplectic with rage. Billy puts out a hand to steady him.

Whizzer: You fucking foreigners have stole the lot.
(cont'd) There ain't no fucking houses left for us,
You dirty mother-fucking load of pus—

Billy: —come off it, son, he didn't mean—

And then Whizzer spits at HE. The gob of spit lands expertly on his target. Whizzer looks triumphant.

HE stands very, very still, for a long moment, looking down at his hands.

HE: Boy—answer me—are your hands clean?

Whizzer: I'm not an Arab if that's what you mean.

HE gestures at his crotch, smiling wickedly, coldly.

HE: Then you may touch...

Whizzer: This fuck's too fucking much!

HE: Insult my people, you're insulting me.
(enraged) I may have my doubts, but now when I see
An animal like you I'd rather be
A man of any faith than be of none.

Billy, meanwhile, has abandoned his role as peacemaker.

Billy: Go on then Whizzer, give it to him, son.

Whizzer pulls away from Billy, picks up a heavy frying pan and rushes at HE.

HE lifts his knife instinctively in self-defence. Everyone freezes. There is a sudden awful silence in the kitchen.

A CCTV camera records the moment.

And then Management appears in the kitchen in the form of a short man wearing a Father-Christmas hat and a smart suit. All eyes are on HE who stands alone, brandishing his long, gleaming, lethal-looking knife.

Manager: Out!

HE looks around the kitchen, at the fear etched in everyone's faces. Then he slowly turns the knife around, hands it quietly to the manager, and walks out.

House / Drawing Room – Night

Anthony is working on some papers whilst listening, as usual to his favourite blues. He starts moving, awkwardly, to the beat, and then can hold still no longer and plays air-guitar to a soaring guitar solo, gradually becoming lost in the music and in his fantasy.

Laboratory – Night

SHE is in her laboratory, deserted apart from a cleaner pushing a broom slowly across the floor. SHE is dialling a number repeatedly on her mobile phone.

Alleyway – Night

HE is walking rapidly through a dark alleyway amongst mountainous sacks of rubbish. His mobile phone rings, its shrill tones echoing in the darkness.

HE pulls the phone out of his pocket, angrily.

> SHE: I need to see you.
> *(v.o.)*

> HE: Look, I can't, not now.
> *(irritated)*

> SHE: Then later?
> *(v.o.)*

> HE: No.

Silence.

> SHE: Tomorrow, anyhow?
> *(v.o.)*

> HE: I cannot say.

> SHE: You cannot say, why not?
> *(v.o., bristling)*

> HE: Some problems.

Laboratory – Night

SHE is pacing backwards and forwards in the laboratory with her mobile phone pressed to her ear.

> SHE: Well, me too...have you forgot?
> Look, we need to talk. Let's go away.
> A small hotel, a night or two. I'll pay.

She hears a mutter of disgust, and then the line going dead as he snaps it shut. She stares at the mobile phone in her hand; she looks baffled, confused, hurt.

House / Drawing Room – Night

Anthony completes his air-guitar solo, falling ecstatically (and heavily) onto his knees on the white carpet.

Laboratory – Night

The music continues as the cleaner pushes her broom silently across the floor past the camera.

Tube Train – Night

HE sits, slumped, in the brightly lit carriage of an underground tube train as it hurtles noisily through the dark tunnels under the city.

House / Dining Room – Night

SHE is sitting waiting silently, immobile, at an immaculate polished table laid for two in the dining room. The white lights on a silvery white Christmas tree are flashing on and off at the far end of the room. Anthony eventually appears and sits down opposite her. There is a long tense pause before either of them moves or speaks.

Anthony:	Sorry.

SHE:	How are you?

Anthony:	Fine.

Silence.

SHE:	That's it?

Anthony: *(quietly)*	Don't nag.

SHE:	I'm sorry, I don't follow you.
	Could you repeat? Or is it that I ought
	To learn somehow to read your mind?
	I'm sure that if I try I'll find
	A way....

Anthony puts down his soup spoon with an angry gesture and stands up.

Anthony:	I'm going out.

He starts to walk towards the door, hesitates, then turns around and looks at her coldly.

Anthony: *(cont'd)*	Sometimes you are a bitch.

SHE: *(sarcastically)*	The bitch and nag: a lovely pair.
	Yes, do go out and get some air.

She gets up abruptly and shouts at him, gesturing angrily.

SHE: *(cont'd, shouting)*	Why won't you fight? Why won't you shout?
	Then we could argue our way out.

Anthony: *(quietly)*	Look...as it happens, I am proud
	Of my control. You say out loud

The first thing that occurs to you.

SHE disappears out of sight into the hallway.

Anthony: *(cont'd)*	I don't behave like you and I Am glad of that. I try To do my best for us.

She sighs, noisily, off-screen.

Anthony: *(cont'd)*	Don't sigh...

SHE: *(o.s., shouting)*	Am I too much? Am I too real? Perhaps with me you have to feel.

He stares at her.

Anthony:	Feel what? The loss of all our dreams? The end of us?

He walks away from her into the drawing room, muttering.

Anthony: *(cont'd, o.s.)*	Some empty schemes To fill the void...re-decorate The house perhaps, or celebrate My birthday or some other date....

He stares at himself in the mirror.

Anthony: *(cont'd)*	*Our anniversary! Let's wake* *Up somewhere else. Let's take a break,* *Lie on a beach and feel the ache* *Of emptiness. You're bored, you read* *A book. And then we go and feed* *Ourselves at some expensive place* *You hate, and so you pull a face* *At me as if the fault were mine.*

She is leaning against the door-frame in the hallway watching Anthony as he stares at his reflection. And then, suddenly, he marches up to her and speaks passionately.

Anthony: You think it's good to feel I've failed?
(cont'd)   You think it's good to feel I've jailed
You, somehow, in a boring, cold
Hell of a place where we grow old
Together, wishing that we weren't?

He turns away, trying to bring his feelings under control.

Anthony: I've learned that not to feel at all is best.
(cont'd)

SHE stares at him.

SHE: *There was a time when love was there.*

And then SHE and Anthony are embracing softly, tenderly, passionately. Is this a memory?

SHE: *There must have been. Yes. It was you*
(cont'd,   *Who once said conversation was*
quietly)   *An aphrodisiac...because*
It flowed. Like nectar, or like juice.

And then they are in the present once more, coldly facing each other across the room.

SHE: Oh, fuck it, fuck it...what's the use.
(cont'd)

SHE turns away with a gesture of hopelessness, walks back to the dining room table and sits down, heavily.

Anthony is about to leave the room but stops, briefly, in the doorway as if he has remembered something. His expression changes.

Anthony: And how is your aunt?
(quietly)

SHE: I...I don't know.

Anthony: You didn't call?

SHE: Not yet—

Anthony: —you're so—

SHE: —So what?

Anthony: Neglectful. Don't you care?

She jumps up, enraged.

SHE: Of course I do! Oh don't you dare
(shouting)   Accuse me. Fuck. Of course I care.
I care too much. I love my aunt.
I'll call right now—oh fuck, I can't—
It's far too late—but, anyhow....

And at last it comes out.

SHE: How could you say those things to Grace?
(cont'd)

The door slams violently.

Streets and Churches – Night

HE is walking in the empty dark streets.

HE stops outside a church with an illuminated nativity scene. He hesitates, and then walks up the steps and stares down at the painted statues. Baby Jesus in a crib. Mary and Joseph. And the three wise men from the East; one of them Arabic, dark skinned, wearing a turban.

House / Bathroom – Night

SHE is sitting on the edge of the lavatory, obsessively dialling a number on her mobile phone. No answer. No answer. She stares at the phone, then punches out the number again.

Apartment – Night

HE is pacing about in his apartment. HE looks dishevelled, angry, unshaven, as he folds clothes and drops them into a suitcase, which lies open on the bed. His mobile phone is ringing. At first he picks it up but when he sees on the screen who is calling, he throws it down again.

House / Bathroom – Night

HE has responded, at last, to her repeated calls.

> *SHE:* What's going on?
>
> *HE:* I can't go on like this.
> *(v.o.)*
>
> *SHE:* Like what? What did I say? What did I miss?
> I need you, need your body, need it so....
> What's wrong? And don't ring off again. Don't go.
>
> *HE:* This is impossible.
> *(v.o.)*
>
> *SHE:* What is? Tell me!

Silence.

> *HE:* Look in your heart and you will surely see
> *(v.o.)* That I have...acted...with sincerity.
> But now the time has come to say...

HE pauses. She holds her breath.

> HE: ...good-bye.
> *(v.o., softly)*

> SHE: What? To say what?

She gasps, groping for words.

> SHE: You can't...but...why?
> *(cont'd)*

Car Park – Night

SHE is at the wheel of her car driving into a bleak deserted city car park. HE is sitting, immobile, in the passenger seat. The car comes to a halt and they sit in silence, each lost in their own thoughts.

HE turns to her and speaks, quietly.

> HE: My body's been in your possession. Now
> I'm asking for it back. It once was mine.
> But, everything I said was true. Oh, how
> I've worshipped you. Yes, you have
>   been...divine.

She stares at him, suspiciously.

> SHE: I'm hearing something strange behind
> Your honeyed words; I feel a doubt
> So strong it's poisoning my mind.
> This bitter question must come out....

But she's struggling.

> SHE: Asking's way beneath me, brother,
> *(cont'd)* For you said there was no other
> One for you. I was your secret country,
> Land of all your longings...so...who is she?

HE shakes his head and sighs.

> HE: No female body tempts me. Please believe
> Me when I say that I would never leave
> You for another woman. Who could be
> The scarlet goddess you have been for me?

HE leans towards her, as if to kiss her, and she moves towards him reciprocally. But he turns away from her, coldly, at the last moment. She stares at him, uncomprehendingly.

Then she gets out of the car, furiously, and slams the door, pacing about as she tries to control herself, her overlapping thoughts and feelings spilling out into fragments of speech.

> SHE: *Ah, but I never asked for this...*
> (murmuring) Ah, but I never asked for this...
> *To be blinded groping for a kiss...*
> To be blinded groping for a kiss...
> My mind's on fire....
> *Where once my limbs coiled with desire*
> *For you, now all I feel is hate.*

HE gets out of the car and stands, silently, watching her as she walks back and forth, angrily.

> SHE: I want to attack.
> (cont'd) *I want to stab you, fucker, in the back.*
> *And make you feel the power of my vengeance....*
> Sweet-talking man with your...hypocrite romance.

> HE: A hypocrite? I'm not the lying kind.
> What can I do to purify your mind?
> I need to...wash you—yes—from head to toe....

She stares at him.

> SHE: What did you say?

HE: How can you doubt me so?

SHE: Wash me? Do you see some dirt?
        Can you not see how your words hurt?

HE: Divinity—

SHE: —don't call me that. It isn't me.

HE: In long afternoons I've felt your lovely arms
        About me, tasted you, and known the charms
        Of flesh on flesh, of skin on lovely skin.
        But when your blood is calling it's a sin—

SHE: —Now wait. Blood? Sin? What's happening?

HE: I have remembered who I am. The old
        And wisest men explain that all the love
        A woman gives distracts us. We are told
        That riches wait for those who rise above
        Temptation to obey a higher call.
        You're asking me to turn away, to fall
        From grace....

SHE: You cannot look me in the face
        And say I am your fall from grace.

They stare at each other, wordlessly, for a moment. Then SHE turns away and starts gesturing, angrily, as she speaks.

SHE: Do you really think that I am unclean?
(cont'd) A second-hand cunt, a fucking machine?
        A dirty distraction, somehow...obscene?
        Look: I'm not only your "goddess" or "queen,"
        I'm a twenty-first century any damn thing
        That I choose; including your teacher or king!

HE: I named you goddess and queen! I crowned you!
(shouting)

SHE: Fuck you! Who do you think you are?
(shouting)

HE: I draw a line:
    You're not a king. That role is mine.

SHE: Oh, sir, excuse me, I forgot:
    You are a son and I am not.
    I am a daughter, so, inferior?

HE: It's you—your people—feel superior.
    You want to rule, you want to spoil;
    You want our land, you want our oil....
    You call that civilised?
    Your country is a dragon, breathing flames;
    Land of corporate fantasies, brand names;
    Big Mac, big burger, yes, big everything.
    And you, blonde American, are too thin,
    Too fit, not womanly. And then, your skin:
    Too pale, insipid. And your eyes, too blue.
    Why do you make me dream of you?

She stares at him, bewildered, hurt, despairing.

SHE: So, we...are at war.
    Oh...you...terrorist....

HE: Imperialist!

SHE: Bigot!

HE: Bitch!

They look at each other for a long silent moment.

SHE: How did it come to this?
You are confusing me with them.
Look, I'm not just an American.
I'm Irish too.

HE: So what?
You all have roots somewhere, but have forgot
That you are anything but powerful.
The big boss.

HE stares at her, coldly.

HE: You hear our children's screams but feel no loss
(cont'd) Because they are not yours.

SHE: That isn't fair.
The things they've done have not been in my name.
I don't feel pride. I feel a deepening shame.

She is desperate now. She comes close to him, looks him in the eye.

SHE: Look, I'm an individual. I am me.
(cont'd)

HE: Me this, me that. Each one of us is we.
We're not alone.

SHE: I know. Look, I agree.
I'm not your enemy. How did this start?

HE: From Elvis to Eminem, Warhol's art,
(wearily) I know your stories, know your songs by heart.
But do you know mine? No, every time,
I make the effort, and I learn to rhyme
In your English. And do you know a word
Of my language, even one? Have you heard
That "al-gebra" was an Arabic man?
You've read the Bible. Have you read the Koran?

54

SHE: Is this the reason you're rejecting me?
(softly)

  HE: Rejection? No. I don't reject.
          But, yes, I do demand respect.

HE struggles with himself before he can continue to speak.

    HE: You say you want me.
(cont'd)   But as what? Your exotic, something other?
          Your toy-boy, pet, your secret lover?

She is gazing at him. He glances at her, pauses, and then...

    HE: You buy me with a credit card
(cont'd)   In restaurants. You want me hard
          So you can melt. Why can't you see
          That being wanted, not for me,
          Not for my noble ancestry,
          But for my flesh, erodes my dignity.
          Your pride is hurt, you're feeling small
          And wounded. But can I walk tall
          When people spit into my face
          Because they fear me? Where's my place
          Of pride and honour in this game
          Where even to pronounce my name
          Is an impossibility?

She is listening intently now, with a soft, open expression.

  SHE: I hear you. Tell me more.
(softly)

*And now the tears are spilling out of his eyes and rolling down his cheeks.
HE struggles to get the words out.*

    HE: In your land...
          I am not seen. I am...un-manned.
          You can't imagine with the white-

Skinned sense of privilege and human rights
You take for granted, how I fight
For every little thing....

*And then her phone rings. She hesitates, and then takes it out of her
pocket, reluctantly. Her expression changes as she listens.*

SHE: Oh no. Oh no, oh no.

She turns to him, panic-stricken, and then rushes away towards her car.

SHE: I have to go.
(cont'd)   I didn't call. I didn't call.
Oh why didn't I call?

*She gets into her car, slams the door, and drives off. HE slowly squats
down on his haunches, his head in his hands, his shoulders shaking, as he
weeps silently in the empty echoing car park. Dawn is breaking, the cold
morning light creeping across the concrete floor.*

Taxi (Belfast) – Day

*The sound of a jet plane passing overhead as SHE stands by some red-
bricked houses at a crossroads of some narrow streets in Belfast. And then
she is sitting in a taxi driving through the city; past the long, grim, walls
that divide one part of the community from the other; walls topped with
barbed wire and covered with graffiti. The taxi pulls up outside a nursing
home, a massive Victorian building set in walled grounds, dominated by a
crucifix.*

Nursing Home – Day

*Nuns in white habits are pushing elderly people in wheelchairs down long
corridors. There are some desultory Christmas decorations hanging from
the walls.*

*She walks slowly along a corridor and then stops just outside the entrance
to a ward and leans back against the wall to prepare herself. She closes
her eyes as we hear her aunt's voice for the first time.*

Aunt: *You're late again. Don't worry. Never mind.*
          I know you're busy. It's the kind
          Of life you lead. But then you chose it, so
          I guess you want it. Always to and fro,
          You never stop.

SHE tiptoes into the ward and stands looking down at her aunt who lies immobile, her eyes closed, in the bed.

Aunt: *Unlike myself. I'm here*
(cont'd)   *To stay. For just how long, who knows, I fear*
          It could be ages. It creeps up on you,
          This funny business. First a creak or two,
          Your knees, perhaps, and—bingo!—then you're old
          And in a bed.

SHE kisses her aunt's forehead, gently pulls up a chair and sits down by the bed.

SHE: Oh, auntie....
(whispering)

Aunt: *The thing is, no-one told*
          Me I'd have all this time, but far too late
          To use it for the things I dreamed of. Fate
          Delivers upside down and back to front.
          I've more to say than ever, but they shunt
          Me back and forth all day from bed to chair
          And back to bed again; it isn't fair.
          All this experience I'd like to share.
          Not that it all adds up. Not that you care.
          I'd better stop—it's time for you to go
          Already, isn't it? Five minutes—oh,
          Well maybe ten...you see, I never know
          When you'll be here again. It's such a blow
          Each time you leave, it's hardly worth your while
          To come at all. I mean it! Don't you smile
          Like that! Oh, you'll be sorry when I'm dead.

I'm only joking, dear. I only said
That for a laugh. Although of course it's true.
The questions that you never asked...yes, you
Will certainly regret a thing or two.

A smiling Father Christmas, dressed traditionally in a red snow-suit, with a huge white beard and carrying a sack of gifts, appears in the doorway. SHE signals politely for him to leave. He turns and shuffles away.

    Aunt: No one explained to me when I was young
   (cont'd) Why time only goes forward. Hold your tongue
              Was what they said when I asked them about
              The universe and such and why we can't
              Do all that much about it when we make
              A mess of things. If only a mistake
              Could be corrected. Wind life back and start
              Again. The second time we'd know the art
              Of living. But we only get one go;
              No dress rehearsals, this one is the show,
              And we don't know it. I don't see the rhyme
              Or reason in this so-called grand design....

And now it is a priest who enters the ward, quietly, and rapidly gives her aunt the last rites, making the sign of the cross above her and softly muttering a prayer.

    Aunt: But then I don't believe. There is no sign
   (cont'd) Of him up there as far as I'm concerned.
              See...if there's one thing that I've truly learned
              It's this: it's down to me.

Her eyes flicker open as the priest leaves the ward. SHE leans forward and smiles tenderly at her aunt.

    Aunt: And you, of course.
   (cont'd)

Her aunt's eyes are trying to focus on her face.

Aunt:	Each one of us is it; we are the source
(cont'd)	Of all the bad...and of the good things too.
	But—out with it—what's happening with you?
	At last you've got some colour in your cheeks.
	I haven't seen you look this way in weeks
	Or maybe months. It even could be years.
	Don't tell me...you're in love, aren't you my dear?

Her eyes close again. SHE gets up and paces back and forth at the end of the bed as her aunt's voice continues over.

Aunt:	Not with that English chap. What a mistake!
(cont'd)	I knew it from the start. It only takes
	Another one to come along, and then
	Your heart tells you that, frankly speaking, men
	Are not all equal—some are better, love.
	It's just another trick from that one up above—
	If He exists, which He—or She—does not—
	Unless I didn't notice—or forgot—
	But I've a perfect memory! I lie
	Here running through the lot. I think I'll die
	With all that information tucked away.
	I'd trade in all of it for just one day—

And then—suddenly—she speaks out loud for the first time.

Aunt:	—In Cuba.
(cont'd)	

SHE startles at the sound of her aunt's voice, suddenly strong and strident, and rushes back to the bed.

SHE:	Auntie? What did you say?

But her aunt is exhausted from the effort of speaking out loud.

Aunt:	You heard me. Cuba. Oh, I'd love to see
	The place; the people, the reality
	Of how it all turned out.

> And Castro...gave us hope
> He did. Oh yes, he's better than the Pope....
> I'd love to shake his hand.

Silence. And then, with an effort, her aunt suddenly focuses on her and speaks out loud again.

> Aunt: You should go soon.
> (cont'd)

> SHE: Yes...yes...

SHE is really close to her aunt's face now, willing her to speak once more, but her aunt has closed her eyes and drifted off again.

> Aunt: I tell you, we'll be living on the moon
> Before we have another go like that.
> A great big dream that's fallen pretty flat
> In all the other countries where they tried
> It. They'll regret it. Communism died,
> But what came in its place? A load of greed.
> A life spent longing for things you don't need.

Nursing Home / Corridor – Day

SHE leaves the ward and walks down the long corridor, past a cleaner who is mopping the floor.

She stands by a Christmas tree, pulls her mobile phone out of her bag, and starts to punch out a number. Then she pauses for a moment, distracted by a nun hurrying towards her and beckoning urgently. She shuts off her mobile phone and runs back to her aunt's ward.

The cleaner watches them disappear and then turns, slowly, to look into the camera.

Nursing Home / Ward – Day

Her aunt has died while she was out of the ward. Two nuns are arranging

*her body, folding her arms, closing her eyes. SHE sits down, slowly and
heavily, grief-struck, by the bed.*

*Time seems to slow down, as she weeps, silently, wordlessly. But she is
listening—listening to her aunt, who seems to be speaking to her from the
other side, in a low, rapid litany.*

Aunt: *If and when I die*
I want to see you cry
I want to see you tear your hair
Your howls of anguish fill the air
I want to see you beat your breast
And rent your clothes and all the rest
And, sobbing, fall upon my bed...
I want to know that I am dead.

I want to know I'm part of you
And that you cannot bear me being torn away
I want to see you dressed in black
With red-rimmed eyes
From sleepless nights of grieving
I want to hear you protest
At me leaving
I want to see you in each other's arms
And wailing
See you kick a chair and punch the wall
And see you, moaning, fall
Upon the ground and scream....
I want to know this isn't just a dream.

I want my death to be just like my life
I want the mess, the struggle, and the strife
I want to fight and see you fight for me
I want to hear your last regrets
The things you wish you'd done and said
—In fact I'd like that just before I'm dead—
Don't let them put you off
Or make you go, or say it's bad

For me, or makes it hard for me to leave....
It won't be true. I want to see you grieve.

Don't let me drown in silence
All pious and polite
Let's make a lot of noise!
A different kind of light
Will fill the room.
I want my death to wake you up
And clean you out
And as I end
I'll hear you shout....

SHE gives in to her own grief at last and throws herself upon her aunt's body.

SHE: No, no!
(wailing)

Aunt: *But I will go.*

SHE: No, no! Please don't die....

SHE is sobbing, now, her tears flowing freely, waiting for a response that never comes.

Nursing Home / Lobby – Day

SHE is standing in the lobby of the nursing home next to a Christmas tree, her eyes red-rimmed, talking urgently into her mobile phone.

SHE: Life is so short and precious. Let's not waste
What we've been given. Look—we have not faced
The truth; even the rages we express
Perhaps contain the seeds of happiness.
Let's go...let's go to Cuba—

HE: —What?
(v.o.)

SHE: —Far away
   From everyone. We've never spent a day
   And night together, only an hour or two;
   Let's take the time for us: just me and you....

There is a silence at the other end of the phone, but she can hear the sound of traffic, cars honking and unfamiliar music.

Streets (Beirut) – Day

HE is standing in blazing sunshine holding his mobile phone to his ear, surrounded by the wounded, shrapnel-scarred buildings of Beirut.

  HE: I'm in Beirut.

There is a long pause.

  SHE: You are?
  (v.o.)

  HE: I have a friend—
    We trained and worked together. In the end
    He stayed, he's married, now he has a son....

Nursing Home / Lobby – Day

She cannot contain herself any longer.

  SHE: There's only one
  (v.o.) Life. This is it. Let's seize the time. I'll send
    A ticket to you....I'll go on ahead....
    My auntie died. She died. My aunt is dead.

  HE: It's many years....
  (v.o.)

HE is silent. And then she completes his sentence for him.

....since you've been there?
(quietly)   You'll have a lot to say. A lot to share.
I'll send the ticket anyway.

Streets (Beirut) – Day

The conversation has ended. HE turns and walks across the dusty wasteland as the muezzin calls the faithful to prayer through the distorting loudspeakers in the distance.

Nursing Home / Ward – Day

SHE is sitting in a chair, exhausted, immobile, as her aunt's body is wheeled out of the room by two nuns.

House / Kitchen – Day

The cleaner is crouching by the open door of the oven in the spotless, immaculate, under-used kitchen of her employers' house. She looks cheerful and calm. She has something to explain as she scrapes some grease from the oven door with her fingernail.

Cleaner: Dirt doesn't go, it just gets moved around.
(to camera)   Some things get burnt, or buried in the ground,
But fire makes smoke and soot and greasy grime
And buried stuff crops up after a time....

Kate's House / Grace's Bedroom – Night

Grace is doing her homework, lying on her bed. She gets up and stares disgustedly at herself in the mirror, pulling in her stomach, punching her flesh, and weeping.

Cleaner: It travels slowly—one could say it creeps—
(v.o.)   It's all the water underneath...it seeps.

God gave us eyes that do not see too much
Or we'd go mad....

House / Drawing Room – Day

The cleaner has moved through to the drawing room and plumps up some cushions on a sofa.

Cleaner: We'd never want to touch
A bed again, a sofa or a chair,
If we could see the things that live in there.
There's millions of them; loads of things with legs.
They fornicate and then they lay their eggs.
They think our dirt is lovely; they survive
By eating what we shed. They are alive
'Cause bits of us are dead....

House / Bedroom – Night

Anthony is lying in the marital bed, gazing unhappily into the distance. A female hand appears, caressingly, on his shoulder, and starts to pull him toward her.

House / Bathroom – Day

The cleaner has moved into the bathroom and is scrubbing the bathtub with a toothbrush.

Cleaner: Now, smaller than
The mites are germs. Well, we do what we can;
We scrub and scrub, but they fly when we sneeze,
On drops of moisture, packed out with disease.
Then all we have to do is take a breath
And they're inside us, fighting to the death.
It's not just germs. It seems they're not the worst.
There's viruses. Some say they were the first
Things to exist. And 'cause they are so small

They can't be cleaned away, no, not at all,
Not ever. That's why, really, in the end
There's no such thing as spotless. You just send
The dirt to somewhere else, push it around....

Embassy / Kitchen – Night

The three kitchen workers are standing silently in the deserted kitchens. Billy is cleaning up, carefully wiping down a surface. He bends down and looks into the camera.

> *Cleaner:*　The work is endless, that is what I've found.
> *(v.o.)*

House / Dressing Room – Day

The cleaner is lying on the floor of the mirrored dressing room, picking up small pieces of fluff from the carpet.

> *Cleaner:*　Maybe this earth is just a ball of fluff.
> Some great big cleaner out there said: enough,
> And that is how we all survived. Why not?
> We're just the parasites that God forgot.

Embassy / Kitchen – Night

Virgil, Billy and Whizzer turn in unison and stare into the camera, silently.

House / Dressing Room – Day

The cleaner, still lying on the carpet, moves even closer to the camera and speaks urgently.

> *Cleaner:*　The point is this; we never disappear,
> Despite it being what we all most fear.
> We're certainly not finished when we die,
> However hard the undertakers try.

Every single creature feeds another.
Everyone is everybody's mother...
Or, at the very least, a kind of host.
When we expire perhaps we change, at most,
But never vanish.

House / Bedroom – Day

The cleaner plumps up a pillow on her employers' immaculate white bed.

> *Cleaner:*   No—we leave a stain.
> A fingerprint. Some mess. Perhaps some pain....

House / Bedroom – Night

Anthony has rolled over into the welcoming arms of the woman in his bed.
They embrace. It is Kate (the friend SHE went running with in the park,
the mother of Grace).

> *Cleaner:*   Some fear, or doubt in someone else's heart.
> *(v.o.)*

Kate's House / Kate's Bedroom – Day

Grace slowly opens the door of her mother's bedroom.

> *Grace:*   Mum?

Grace peers into the bedroom. It is empty. She leans back against the
door, weeping.

House / Bedroom – Day

The cleaner now lies down on the bed she has been making, her head on
the white pillow, and looks into the camera.

Cleaner: We leave a mess, in fact, when we depart.
(softly)

Streets (Havana) – Day

Wide busy streets, crumbling buildings, huge battered American cars, bicycles, rickshaws, people, noise, heat and music. This is Cuba.

Room (Havana) – Day

SHE is being shown into a shabby room by an older woman; blue walls, a bed, a couple of chairs.

SHE glances around the room. She looks exhausted; hot, sweaty, un-made-up.

She puts down her suitcase, slowly takes off her shoes and sits on the bed with an expression of relief. Then she closes her eyes.

Streets (Beirut) – Night

HE is walking through the dark narrow streets of a shantytown in Beirut. Men wave at him from doorways. HE passes some small boys kicking a football and briefly joins in with their game.

Room (Havana) – Day

SHE stands looking out of the window at the hot busy streets, then moves slowly back into the room, sits down in a rocking chair and closes her eyes, rocking gently.

Streets (Beirut) – Night

HE walks down a narrow alley towards his friend, who is waiting for him. They fall into each other's arms.

*And then his friend calls his wife, a young dark-eyed woman, who hugs
and kisses her husband's long-lost companion.*

Discotheque (Havana) – Night

*SHE is being asked to dance by a man in a crowded discotheque. Intensely
loud salsa music is playing. A montage of moments follows as she dances
with one man after another, her hair gradually falling down, her face
lighting up, her body relaxing. The sound of the salsa becomes...*

Room (Beirut) – Night

*A muezzin is calling the faithful to prayer, amplified through distorting
loudspeakers, somewhere in the sleeping city. HE is sitting, immobile, on
the edge of his bed, his expression inscrutable. After a while he gets up,
goes into the bathroom, splashes his face with cold water and stares at
himself in the mirror.*

Clinic (Beirut) – Day

*HE is being shown into a small, impoverished clinic by his friend. The
facilities look meagre, but clean. And then, covered with a green cloth,
there are the surgeon's instruments, including a scalpel.*

*HE picks the scalpel up, familiarly, the way he had picked up his knives in
the embassy kitchen.*

Church (Beirut) – Day

*HE is standing, holding a baby boy, at the baptism in a packed Armenian
church in Beirut. The ceremony has just finished and throngs of people
are coming forward to pin money and gold trinkets on to the baby's white
satin robes.*

*Cameras are flashing. A video is being made. HE smiles for the video
cameraman, blinking in the glare of his lights, then points into the camera,
and waves.*

Restaurant (Beirut) – Day

The video cameraman is filming the happy crowd who are sitting at tables, talking, laughing and eating. The friend of HE is holding his newborn son, proudly. The blurry video image becomes...his friend and his wife dancing together joyfully, as the crowd claps in time with the music. HE sits, quietly, and watches them dance.

His friend crosses the floor and invites him to join them. HE protests, but is finally persuaded. HE dances for a while with his friend's wife, trying to look happy, but he looks tired and alienated. Eventually HE sits down again, lost in thought.

Streets and Malecon (Havana) – Day

SHE is riding in the back of an ancient convertible, filming street-life in Havana with a small video camera; the balconies hung with washing, the huge battered American cars, bicycles, dogs, a wedding procession. And then the seafront (the Malecon) where people gather to pass the time of day. The sea glitters in the background. People are lying on the sea wall; children are playing on the rocks and shouting in the blazing sunshine; a lone trumpeter practices into the wind.

A huge wave suddenly breaks over the wall.

And now SHE is running along the city seafront, the blue sky and sea behind her. Images of faces in the marketplace, flower stalls, cobblers working, women shopping, are super-imposed over her image as she runs and runs, hot and happy, somehow released from sorrow and tension.

Room / Bathroom (Havana) – Day

SHE runs into the bathroom of the apartment where she is staying, panting and sweating, and then she splashes her face with water, laughing.

Room (Havana) – Day

SHE places her small video camera on a low cupboard opposite the bed.

The camera records glimpses of her face in the lens as she bends down to check that everything is as it should be. Then she walks to the bed, sits down and looks into the camera.

SHE: God, if you exist...I need to confess.
(to camera)

Silence. She hesitates, then stops speaking out loud and sits back with a sigh.

SHE: *Please speak to me, just once. Don't make me guess*
(cont'd)   *Your point of view, for I might get it wrong.*

The video camera records her as she gets up and moves restlessly about the room, then sits down again on the bed, staring out of the window, occasionally glancing back into the camera.

SHE: *I know I've strayed so far I don't belong*
(cont'd)   *In any church of yours. I've sung the song*
Of science. Yes, I've sung it every day.
But, I could argue, that is how I pray...
For twenty years—god, can it be?
I've cut, dissected; carefully
And with respect. Each living cell
A source of wonder, as I tried to see...
To penetrate your mystery.
The point is, God, you never lie.
But you have secrets. So have I.
Now all I was has turned to ash and doubt,
For love has tasted me and spat me out.
At first there's blossom, then there is decay....
Impermanence will never go away.
In fact it is the only certainty;
There'll come a time when I will cease to be....
But not quite yet.

She stands up, decisively, crosses the room, rewinds the tape, then sits back down on the bed and speaks out loud again, looking directly into the lens once more.

> SHE:
> (cont'd, to
> camera)
>
> Oh God...can you forgive me
> For not—for not believing in you?

She stares silently, questioningly, into the lens and then hears a woman shouting to her from outside.

> Woman:
> (o.s.)
>
> Signora!

> SHE:
>
> Si?

> Woman:
> (o.s.)
>
> Un senor.

SHE looks questioningly into the camera. Can it be?

Room (Havana) – Day

SHE moves slowly through the room towards the doorway. Yes, it is him. HE walks towards her. And then, back in her bedroom, he lies down, exhausted, his head falling into her lap. She looks down at him, tenderly, and strokes his hair. After a while she looks up at the window, towards the light.

Beach (Havana) – Day

HE and SHE are rolling on the sand, kissing, laughing, gazing at each other with love, tenderness and joy.

As they kiss, the image freezes and becomes a cell, quivering, vibrating...until suddenly, beautifully and magically, it divides.

> Cleaner:
> (v.o.)
>
> When you look closer, nothing goes away.
> It changes, see, like night becomes the day
> And day the night; but even that's not true:
> It's really all about your point of view,
> Depending where you're standing on the earth....

The dividing cell then becomes the word "YES" traced in the sand. The letters gradually disappear, washed away by the encroaching tide.

Here are the images we have been glimpsing throughout the story; a landscape of life forms at the smallest visible level, where all is undeniably inter-connected.

Cleaner: And, in the end, it simply isn't worth
(cont'd)   Your while to try and clean your life away.
    You can't. For everything you do or say
    Is there, forever. It leaves evidence.

House / Bedroom – Day

The cleaner is lying on the bed where we saw her last, looking into the camera.

Cleaner: In fact it's really only common sense;
    There's no such thing as nothing, not at all.
    It may be really very, very small
    But it's still there. In fact I think I'd guess
    That "no" does not exist. There's only "yes."

She looks silently into the camera and then slowly turns her head away.

The end credits begin.

But we return twice to the cleaner.

She checks that we are still there, watching her. And then finally, she turns her head into the pillow as a tear rolls down her cheek and she closes her eyes for the last time.

END

Photographs

9

10

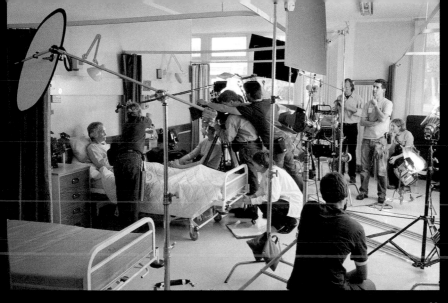

23

24

25

26

Captions for Photographs by
Nicola Dove and Gautier Deblonde

1. The cleaner (Shirley Henderson) in the house
2. Anthony (Sam Neill) and SHE (Joan Allen) in the embassy
3. SHE and HE (Simon Abkarian) in Regent's Park
4. HE and SHE in his apartment
5. The kitchen workers: Virgil (Wil Johnson), Whizzer (Raymond Waring), Billy (Gary Lewis)
6. The swimming-pool cleaner (Barbara Oxley)
7. Grace (Stephanie Leonidas) at the swimming pool
8. HE and SHE in the restaurant
9. Anthony in the house
10. SHE in HE's apartment
11. HE in his apartment
12. The cleaner with Anthony and Grace in the house
13. SHE in the laboratory
14. SHE and Anthony in the house
15. SHE and HE in the car park
16. SHE and her aunt (Sheila Hancock) in the nursing home
17. HE in Beirut
18. Grace in her room
19. HE and SHE in Havana
20. The cleaner in the dressing room
21. Joan Allen and Sally Potter on location, London
22. Simon Abkarian, Joan Allen, Alexei Rodionov (director of photography), Denis Garnier (Focus Puller) on location, Dominican Republic (beach scene, Cuba)
23. Sheila Hancock, Joan Allen, Sally Potter and crew on location, London (nursing home, Belfast)
24. Sally Potter on location, London
25. Simon Abkarian, Joan Allen and Sally Potter on location, London
26. Simon Abkarian on location, London
27. Joan Allen on location, London
28. Joan Allen, Simon Abkarian and Sally Potter on location, London

The Original Five-Minute Script

What follows is the unedited five-minute script, set in Paris, upon which the screenplay of *YES* was based, using the original format and layout.

A woman is walking. Walking down the stairs in her hotel, out onto the pavements, weaving her way through the street market, crossing the road, click-clacking along the pavement. We hear her talk (or is it her thoughts we are listening to?). She speaks so fast, so angrily. We do not see her face, or even her body. We stay close to her feet. Feet in high heels. Scuffed, bruised shoes that were expensive once.

SHE: *(fast and furious)*
No, no, what is this no?
This farewell, sweet, I love you so?
This now it's time to let you go?
This finish, stop, go with the flow
Of ending, with a stab, a blow,
An axe into my heart that I
Might cease to beat and surely die?
Cannot you see the rush of blood?
I feel it gushing in a flood
Of pain and redness. So, I said
I wanted more. But now instead
You want to say goodbye to me
And speak the word so tenderly
As if it were a gift, a feast
Of wisdom coming from the east...
A teaching, about destiny:
Accept, surrender to the one
And only truth, that *you* decide
Is true and I must not deride
'Cause I'm a daughter, you're a son.
I gave you me! I need a gun
To shoot you with; my minds on fire...
Where once my limbs coiled with desire
For you, now all I feel is hate.
Oh lover I can hardly wait
To get my hands on you again;
But not for pleasure, now its pain
I want to give you, that's your fate.

A man is sitting.
Sitting on a seat in a train in
the metro as it sways through
the tunnels deep under the
city. We stay close to his
feet—shiny shoes, patent
leather, so smart—the feet of
a playboy. And we hear his
voice, murmuring, placating,
soft, the seducer's voice. His
accent is broken and his
words are those of a kind
man, a shy man.

As the train stops, the man
rises from his seat and steps
out onto the long deserted
platform.

The woman is now crossing a
busy road. She walks. She
runs. She stumbles. Her feet
express anxiety, but also
energy and direction. Her
feet pass other feet, and dogs,
and water flowing along in
the gutters.

HE: *(slow and calm)*
Silky touch woman weighing on me, how
Your feather fingers have become like lead.
You stroke me and you crush my dignity
To dust—no air, no space around my head.
I need to breathe, to break away from all
The lovely bonds that hold me in your thrall.
This quest for freedom truly does not mean
I have not worshipped you. Oh, perfect queen,
My body's been in your possession, now
I'm asking for it back; it once was mine.
But, even with your heaviness, I vow
You are my empress, majesty divine.

SHE: *(fast, suspicious)*
I'm hearing something strange behind
Your honeyed words; I feel a doubt
So strong it's poisoning my mind.
This bitter question must come out:
Who is she who has grabbed my space?
Usurper, robbed me of my place?
Asking's way beneath me, brother,
For you said there was no other
One for you; I was the lover
You had dreamt of all your days.
You said your eyes, your steady gaze,
Could only fall on me. Your lies
Astound me. Sentiment so fake
And metaphors designed to make
A fool of me. A broken crown
Is all you you've left me, crown of tin;
No precious metal, something thin
And tawdry, only there for show.
Who is she? Where did your love go?

HE: (*slow and lilting*)

The man's feet ride a shining metal escalator, and pass through doors that clang and bang behind him as he steps out into the daylight.

Oh beauty woman, with your eyes like beads
Of jet, and with your beating heart that reads
My senses, laser swift, can I forget
You? Never. But now something calls me, so
I have to end this madness; let me go.
Sweet lover, it's another kind of love
That draws me to her kisses from above.
No female body tempts me, please believe
Me; cherry red princess, I'd never leave
You for another woman; who could be
The scarlet duchess you have been for me?

SHE: (*very fast*)

Those high heels are now crossing an open square, the sound of a fountain playing. Feet balanced on skateboards cross her path—tricks, turns, jumps. Her words are some-times obliterated, cut into new rhythms by the sounds of wheels on stone.

Ah, but I never asked for this:
To be blinded groping for a kiss.
Nobody warned me, nobody said
That losing love is like being dead—
Or deaf and dumb and gagged and strangled—
Your life on hold, your spirit mangled.
But fuck you, love, I'll kill you first,
For what I feel is a terrible thirst;
A thirst for revenge, I'm gonna hit and attack,
I'm gonna stab you, fucker, in the back,
'Cause you're causing havoc in my soul;
This is classical pain, not rock n' roll.
I've a sensation that's more than a feeling:
My body is sick and my mind is reeling,
My spirit's stuck somewhere on the ceiling
And I can't come down, there'll be no healing
Until I've had you in my line of sight
And taught you what it means to fight;
For you haven't felt the power of vengeance,
Sweet-talk man with your hypocrite romance,
Wait till I set my eyes on you, yes,
Wait till I set my eyes on you.

The man's feet, in those patent leather shoes, now are walking on gravel and through piles of drifting leaves. A child rides past on a tricycle. This is the first face we have seen, looking up at the unseen man, curious. The shiny shoes stop and retreat a step or two, and then the man sits on a metal chair, with green grass visible beyond.

HE: *(slow)*

Oh lady luck I want to take your hand
And lead you to the loveliest of lands;
A place I've seen, but only in my dreams.
Beloved, let me bathe you there in streams
Of crystal water, purify your soul,
And pacify your doubting mind. My role
Is clear, I need to wash you head to toe,
Then dry you in the rays of golden sun.
You'll feel the soothing amber nectar flow
Through every part of you, you'll feel it run
In diamond rivulets across your skin.
When you are clean the Lord's work can begin.

Her feet, in those wounded high heels, are running now; gravel under her feet and gravel in her voice.

The child on the tricycle passes again, the small face looking up, curious, at this woman rushing past, oblivious.

SHE: *(fast)*

Wash me? Do you see some dirt?
Cannot you see how your words hurt?
I do not need your abstract jewels.
I need to rewrite all your rules
Of conduct, and the way you think
And speak; and make you drink
The water from *my* wisdom well
And make you listen while *I* tell
You of *my* dreams. Cannot you see
I know the way to ecstasy?
For loving is a kind of prayer
Also, and peels off the layers
Of piety that cloak the soul
And leave us in an empty role
Of goodness and propriety.
Surrender now. Come back to me.

The two voices have collided now, swooping down on each other, his placating poem after her furious words.

HE: *(slow, stubborn)*

Through long dark nights I've felt your
    lovely arms
About me, tasted you, and known the charms
Of flesh on flesh, of skin on lovely skin.
But when the lord is calling it's a sin
To turn away from him, from all the gold

He offers if you follow him. The old
And wisest men explain that all the love
A woman gives distracts us; and we're told
That riches wait for those who rise above
Temptation and obey a higher call.
You're asking me to turn away, to fall
From grace, from ruby wisdom, diamond
    knowledge, all
The treasures only heavenly realms can hold.
Sweet lady of modernity, your bold
And grasping language, frankly, leaves me cold.

SHE: *(fast, enraged)*

Her feet are circling his chair. She stops—shoe to shoe, and then, yes, she treads on his, in rage. He bends down to rub the shiny patent leather; we catch his face, briefly, before he stands. And then she kicks him, her pointy shoes like razor daggers digging into his shin and her words like daggers, too.

I used to feel wealthy, I used to feel rich,
Now you make me feel like a poverty bitch;
A cheap perfume woman, all brassy and bright,
A dame of low dives, living only at night,
Living only for you, for the grace of your touch.
This is driving me mad, this is really too much.
I used to feel shiny and muscle-tone clean;
Now I feel like a second-hand sexual machine—
Dirty and low down and stupid and mean—
But I'm not! I'm not only a goddess and queen
I'm a twenty-first century any damn thing
That I choose; including your teacher or king!

HE: *(after a pause, his anger building)*
I named you goddess and a queen.
I crowned you, it's unseemly for
You now to worship at a throne
Of your own making, in a tone
Of righteous and superior rage.
The vulgar, shocking words you use
To make your point can only lose
You ground. I see you acting out
A mockery of the devout
That serves you ill. This is no play
Of word on word. This is no game.
And now for you to make a claim

79

To be a sage, has gone too far.
You cheapen my beliefs. I met today
With you, at your request, to hear
You out. But now your words I fear
Have forced me, finally, to see
The hard and ugly vanity
You try so hard to hide. Well now
It's clear at last. I will endow
This moment with a final thought;
To dignify this conflict ought
To be my goal. I draw a line:

*And suddenly, he stamps his
foot.*

HE: *(cont.)*
You're not a king! That role is mine!

SHE: *(calmly)*

*There is a silence, for the
first time in this relentless
flood of words. And then the
man turns on his heel and
walks away. She waits for a
moment and then slowly follows, her voice melodious
now, and calm.*

Ah, so now at last the rhythm changes
To a beat that suits the sentiment I
Hear behind your words, and re-arranges
Thought itself. Now let the falsity fly
Away from here. It's time to tell the truth
More ruthlessly than ever. Tell me, now,
What hurt you so, that cold rejection seems
The only answer to affection; dreams
Of higher realms concealing bitterness
So deep, that you're compelled to turn away
From me, the woman who has loved you so

*She falls, slowly, to her
knees. We see her body, now,
but not yet her face.*

Completely. Speak, I'll listen. Tell me how
You're wounded. Maybe I can help to mend
Your broken heart, and so bring to an end
This ghastly war. I'll even call you lord
Of everything—that's better than a king—
I'll flatter you, I'll knight you with a sword,
You'll have no cause to feel your pride is lost
Or damaged by the heat of my desire
For you. You'll realise the only cost
Of sweet surrender is the taste of fire,
The smell of smoke, as flames devour the hard

And brittle shell of you and leave un-marred
The essence; tender, soft. There's nothing higher.

HE: *(hesitant at first, then fast and angry)*
You...you treat me as a lower
Form of life; you say you want me.
But as what? A hot-house flower?
Dark, exotic, something other,
Toy-boy, pet, your secret lover?
You're affronted, that is all.
Your pride is hurt, you're feeling small.
But what of me? Can I walk tall
When people spit into my face
Because they fear me? Where's my place
Of pride and honour in this game
Where even to pronounce my name
Is an impossibility?
Why must I say—why can't you see—
That being wanted, not for me,
Nor for my noble ancestry,
But for my flesh, makes me feel used;
A sensual slave, to be abused.

SHE:
I hear you. Tell me more. I understand
The feeling. Truly. When you speak this way
My rage is silenced. Come now, take the hand
Of friendship I extend to you. The day
Is just beginning....

HE:
In this land
I am not seen. I am un-manned.
You can't imagine with the white-
Skinned sense of privilege and legal rights
You take for granted, how I fight
For every little thing—

He stops in his tracks, hesitates, and then walks back and stands before her.

And then he's on his knees, too, and they fall together onto the green grass, their faces visible at last. Her face is mascara-streaked, it was a long and sleepless night, but she has hair as sleek and glossy as patent leather; and his is a dark and wounded face. And now her voice is placating, and soft, and his are the words of pain, flowing from him as they fall into each other's arms and hair and eyes and mouths.

81

SHE:
—Ah, but I can.
We both are tempest-tossed, and feel the pain
Of what we've lost. And feel so little gain
From all our struggles. Dearest, how I feel
For you, for all of us—

HE:
—Oh sister, mine—

SHE:
—Oh brother, love divine—

HE:
—I want you—

SHE:
—Yes! I'm you, and yours!

HE:
Your breast all perfumed—

SHE:
—Yes! Sweet, come
To me—

HE:
—I'll hold you now for hours
Of love. The joy—

SHE:
—The happiness—
The only word to say is...yes....

Q&A with Sally Potter and Joan Allen

The Q&A that follows is an amalgamation of different sessions at the first festival screenings of *YES*, in Telluride, Toronto, and London. Joan Allen was on stage at some of these. Unlike some directors, I always greatly enjoy these sessions, as I find that the audience teaches me about how the film has worked for them; and therefore what the real relationship is between my intention and the final result. In effect, I discover what I have done; and the things I intended or hoped for fall into place, sometimes in quite surprising ways.

What frequently astonishes me is how consistent the responses to a film are in different countries and the similarities in the questions people ask. What the edited transcripts do not indicate is the emotional reactions of these audiences: the laughter and the tears, the hugs in the aisles of the cinema, the words whispered into my ear, and the questions from those too shy to speak in public.

My thanks are due to all those un-named questioners, both public and private.

Question: What prompted you to make the film at this particular time?

Sally Potter: I started to write the script on 12th September 2001, in direct response to what had happened the day before. What was evident was that there were going to be increasing levels of demonisation of people from the Middle East and reverse levels of hatred of Americans. And so I asked myself: what can I contribute as a filmmaker? I thought a good starting point was a love story between a man from the Middle East and a Western woman, in which love and attraction initially transcend difference, but when world events, history, and national identity can no longer be kept out of the relationship, they have to slug it out.

I started with the scene that eventually became the scene in the car park, which is really the hub of the whole thing. That was the genesis, the initial impulse, let's say. Also, in the way the story would be told, its tone of voice, I wanted to try and make something light in the face of such global heaviness, with optimism and hope embedded in it. And rather than make something didactic about the themes, I decided to go into the hidden emotional currents of both the fear of difference, but also the attraction and love for the other. In short, to make a love story out of a situation full of hate.

Q: Why did you decide to write the script in verse?

SP: The decision to do it in verse felt like an absolutely natural one. It came out that way; it *wanted* to come out that way. It was as if some of the ideas that I wanted to express and have the characters talk about would be hard to say in prose. Much of the film is written in iambic pentameter (ten syllables a line) which some say is close to the rhythm of thought or of breathing, and, in English at least, is a very natural way of speaking. Some of the verse is eight syllables a line, particularly when something direct needs to be said. It's a sharper sort of rhythm.

Apparently sales of poetry go up in times of war. There's a need to be able to hold a distilled phrase in the mind and in the heart rather than prose which just kind of runs and disappears. That is maybe another reason why my instinctive impulse was towards verse. I felt: let's use this marvellous gift that we've been given, the gift of words, and find their sensuality, their strength, and their distillation in the way these characters speak. Let's try and create a Middle Eastern man who's human and rounded, who's complex. Let's create an innocent American woman, who's not supporting the policies of the Bush regime (even though of course in the film—very importantly—she never mentions that directly and nobody mentions 9/11 either. The film is set in the present but the issues the characters are facing have deep historical roots and universal implications). Those were the starting points, those two things: poetry and politics.

Q: Did the poetry come to you easily?

SP: It came out in a torrent. It felt entirely natural as a way of expressing this strange blend of ideas—love and religion and war and death—which otherwise might have become rather heavy and didactic in everyday speech. They were big, big ideas to handle. But something about the form of verse, and iambic pentameter in particular, creates a flow to things that naturalises them.

I think of the film almost like a long song and the song form is something everybody knows. Rap is just one of its more recent incarnations. Poetry is simple and old and direct—from Icelandic sagas and Sanskrit to ballads and hip-hop. Both my experience of writing in verse and the actors' experience of performing it, was that it was liberating. I worked as a song lyricist a lot before, so perhaps that's why, for me, it came naturally.

Q: What were your directions to the actors about how to speak the verse?

SP: Ignore the rhyme, ignore the form, just concentrate on the sense and the emotion. We talked a lot in rehearsal about what it meant, how they felt about it, how it related to their lives and so on. We worked as deeply as we could on rooting the language in their own experience and finding an authentic place from which to speak. In other words to naturalize it as much as possible. So it was a kind of paradox, that having written such a precise holding structure to contain the ideas, we then had to let it go, throw it away, or at least loosen it up. The words were adhered to precisely but there was an irreverent approach to the metre so the rhymes at the end of each line became less noticeable. I've had one or two private screenings where people who knew nothing about the film beforehand didn't even notice it was in verse. So, that was kind of interesting. I like it when people do notice and I like it when they don't.

Q: Why Cuba?

SP: "Why Cuba?"—good title! I think it's a very character-driven moment in the story. The auntie, in her dying reverie, is contemplating what she believed in her life. In fact, all the characters are trying to figure out what they believe; whether God exists or not, which of their dreams and beliefs have fallen, and which have held good. And for the auntie, as she's a radical and an atheist, Cuba represents the last outpost of the communist dream: somewhere on earth where people are put before profit, where the economic system is not based on greed but on a principle of equality. Whatever its failures, however many problems and contradictions there are in Cuba and elsewhere where communism has been tried, for the auntie, it still represents that dream. And in effect it is her dying instruction to her niece: "Go there, go soon. Go before Castro dies, have a look."

It's also, in a way, the only place that these two lovers could finally meet, somewhere other than their own cultures, somewhere at the end of somewhere, this little island of disintegrating hope, where the buildings and the music are so vibrant, so colourful, and so extraordinary.

Q: Was the idea of having your central female character with a background as an Irish Catholic from Belfast there from the very beginning or did that come later on?

SP: It was there from the very beginning. I wanted to create two characters from two conflict zones in the world, who therefore in some sense or other would understand each other. Belfast is one such place and Beirut (where HE comes from) is another. So each of them would have experience of the different kinds of bias, prejudice, and oppression involved in so-called "holy wars." So, that was an important symmetry in the story and, yes, it was there from the beginning.

Q: Can you talk a little about how you approached the visual style of the film?

SP: It evolved over a period of time, in collaboration with our wonderful Russian cinematographer, Alexei Rodionov, who I had previously worked with on *Orlando*. This was our second time working together, and my third with the designer Carlos Conti. We talked about the themes, and we tried to create a look that reflected them. I wanted to find ways of somehow making the camera speak in verse. That meant taking some risks. We experimented, for example, with the effect of shooting at different camera speeds, to find a visual equivalent of the rhythm of the verse in movement; a kind of camera music.

Also, part of the reason for the evolution of this particular visual language was economic necessity. I have so often found that limitation, constraint, or obstacle becomes the engine that powers invention. Originally I was trying to figure out how we could shoot this film without any lights, because there didn't seem to be enough money in the budget to have any. One solution was to shoot at six frames a second, or even three. Later you print each frame four (or eight) times to bring it into sync at twenty-four frames per second. You can shoot almost in the dark, and still see people's faces. I thought it was like a miracle when I discovered it, but I wasn't sure if it would work, so we did some tests and found that it was very beautiful; so I decided to make it part of the language of the film. And then we managed to get some lights as well!

We shot on Super-16mm film stock for the same budgetary reasons and then, after it was edited, it was digitally colour-graded and treated, but most of what you see on the screen was generated in the camera. The way that Alexei shot is more important, I think than the different camera speeds. We called it "searching," searching for the image. Alexei doesn't just look, he *sees*. It's a beautiful quality to work with.

Q: Could you discuss the use of colour in the film, particularly the blue?

SP: Blue, blue sky, blue the sea, blue of her eyes, blue the horizon, the blue room where we ended up, Joan looked good in blue. And blue is considered to be the colour of eternity—what's above and what's beyond. But I think, really, that in the madness of preparing for a shoot and during the shoot itself, all the decisions you make are entirely intuitive. So this is my analysis after the event, but also the beginning of an answer to your question. Colour is important for the film as an expression of the characters' relationship to the world and as the story progresses the film becomes increasingly saturated with colour. Each of the environments that the people live in is a kind of character in its own right with it's own colour palette. That was the basis of all the discussions with Carlos Conti. There's the emotional refrigerator that SHE and her husband, played by Sam Neill, live in; the cold all-white space, which, by the way was a real house in London, with a few things taken out and a few things put in; and then the room that her lover lives in has ochre walls and dark wood and a bit more human mess. Carlos, Alexei, and I discussed these colours and then Carlos and his team applied the paint!

Q: Could you tell us how you shot the extraordinary scene when Joan Allen is at the deathbed of her aunt?

SP: It was a cutting room decision to leave the close-up of Joan at that length (nearly two minutes). When I was shooting I didn't know exactly how I would eventually structure the scene. The close-up was shot at forty-eight frames a second, so it's slow motion, and the camera just looks at Joan's face, feeling her state of loss, the loss of everything that matters to her. Sheila Hancock, who plays the Auntie, was saying her lines off-camera, but because it was shot slow-motion, in effect it was mute; we couldn't use the live sound because it wouldn't be in sync with the picture. In the cutting room I decided that the effect of seeing Joan weep without hearing the sound, and instead hearing what *SHE* was hearing— which was her Auntie's voice from "the other side"—was very powerful. Joan as an actor was an amazing person to work with. She gave me, as a director, the incredible gift of trust and of truly making herself vulnerable and naked, at a kind of soul level, in order to connect with the material. I think that quality is visible in that shot.

Q: Why did you choose for her not to say goodbye to her aunt?

SP: I think, at that point, they're beyond spoken words. But she is listening to her aunt's hidden voice, to her dying thoughts; although of course it is ambiguous whether these are actually her aunt's thoughts or the thoughts she imagines she is having. And, I don't know about you, but I have experienced, as I'm sure many others have, the grief of not having managed to say goodbye to somebody you love before they die; and the longing to hear their voice, just one more time, instead of the terrible finality and silence of death. In this sequence she's having that one last imaginary conversation with her aunt, the one she wishes she'd been able to have. I would urge everyone to do that with the people they love, just in case, and sooner rather than later!

Q: At what point does music composition come into making the movie?

SP: Music is always really important to me in the writing process (as well as in post-production) and I often find myself playing something again and again while I'm writing. In this case it was the Philip Glass piece, "Paru River," played by the Brazilian group Uakti, which appears several times in the film. When we were shooting, I wasn't sure how much music the film could sustain, in addition to the music of the voices. And it took some work in the cutting room to find out what the necessary balance was. In the end I felt it could sustain more than I had predicted. The feeling is that the whole sound world is a score, not just the music, but also the speaking voices. And to balance the amount of dialogue—because there's a lot of it in the film—there also had to be the feeling of silence. I'm sure you noticed that quite a lot of the shots are mute, with just the inner voice of the character speaking. During the Auntie sequence, for example, you see Joan walking but you can't hear her feet, you just hear her auntie's voice. It seemed to me that was something of an equivalent to what happens in your mind in a crisis situation or in a state of great emotional trauma or loss. Your world closes down and the irrelevant sounds disappear. You don't hear your footsteps, you just hear what is important at that moment. It's a kind of emergency state of stream of consciousness and I tried to find an equivalent in the sound world of the film, and the music was a part of that.

I also believe that music can be used in a film as a form of dialogue with the image rather than just underscoring it. I experiment in the cutting room with the effect of many different kinds of music and instrumentation to see what happens. There is a fairly eclectic combination in the final score, from Eric Clapton and B. B. King to Brahms, but what they have in common is supreme musicianship, and also they are in related keys.

Q: Did the story always end the way it does now? It seems like a happy ending.

SP: Well, as all filmmakers know, endings are notoriously difficult to write and this was no exception. I wrote a version in which they came together at the end, I wrote a version where they never came together. I wrote a very, very long sequence (which we filmed) where they talk when he arrives in Cuba and unravel the decisions they've made in their lives. And then they decide that they've really come back together in order to say goodbye, because they're reconciled with the fact that they must let each other go. But the more they talk, the closer they become. Anyway, when I saw it in the cutting room, I said, "Out." No explanations are necessary. In fact for the last ten minutes of the film, they don't need to say a word to each other. I do think that films, to a great degree, are re-written in the cutting room and this was no exception. But I'm happy with the ending. I don't think, however, that it is necessarily a "happy ending" in the conventional sense. We don't know what kind of future these two people are heading towards.

Q: What happens in your director's mind, after the story ends? If you were to do a sequel, where would you go with this?

SP: Well, we did discuss it symbolically. And of course it's impossible not to think about it as a metaphor. He carries with him all the global baggage of the problems of the Middle East. She carries with her the global baggage of the American abroad. And how are the two worlds going to meet? How are we going to survive, hand in hand? But I wanted to create characters that are not mere symbols of the global situation, not just representing an idea, and so I tried to make them living, breathing, and as complex as each and every one of us is. None of the characters in the film is representing only where they come from. They're not holding up a flag, saying Irish, American, or Arabic. I tried to create characters with contradiction in them, who are more than one thing, because that's what many of us are. Nonetheless, these two individuals do carry those layers of meaning. And whilst of course the global problems are certainly not something I as a screen-writer can solve, I did want to end the story on a note of hope. In fact, as a general principle, I feel it to be my responsibility to end a film on a note of hope. It is a choice; but one which observably energises people. We think better, more creatively, and act more decisively from a perspective of hope than from one of despair.

Q: Can we talk about the casting and the process of you and Joan working together?

SP: I think casting is the most important alchemical moment for a director in putting a film together. It's the single most impor-tant decision you make. I've learnt that over the years and now I really take time to get it right (and that puts some demands on the actors who I meet).

I had always enormously respected Joan Allen's delicate, seri-ous, profound performances. She manages to hold a marvellous space where she's a film star, but she hasn't gone with the celebri-ty cult thing in the way that many have. She's a serious actor. She started out in theatre. She's an ensemble player; she loves to be part of a team, part of a group. And she has a very internal quali-ty in her work. When I met her and she started to read, I realised that I had really found the one. There was something about her, not just her technical skills, not just her blondness, her blue-eyedness, which brings with it so much information, so much myth, so much iconography, but somebody who wanted to work from the inside out, and who was prepared to make herself soul-naked for the film—not flesh-naked, we don't need that, although we see some parts of her beautiful body—but the point is, she was prepared to turn herself inside out to root the story and the char-acter in her own life and therefore bring her alive for us. She was really a profound joy to work with.

Joan Allen: You have to feel a certain trust and faith in a person, a director, to feel like you can open yourself up that much and that is not always possible. Sally is really extraordinary in that regard. She sets up an atmosphere of such humanity and shows such interest in the actor's concerns; what's possible, what isn't; let's try it, even if it may not work. There's such an embracing, nonjudgemental quality to Sally that you feel, "I can try this, if it's the worst thing I have ever done, we may learn something, we may know not to go there, or we may find something that's really wonderful," and so it's a lot about Sally's own qualities of openness, not only in her work, but in her life as well.

You can get a sense of that quite immediately, when you meet a person, and I did when she came to my door in New York and we started talking about the script and the character. I knew Simon had already been cast and I knew that the chemistry between the two characters was critical (and if the chemistry didn't work then it shouldn't be me, you know, because without the chemistry between them, there's not a story.) And so we read one of the scenes. Sally was at my kitchen table and Simon was in Paris, and we read a scene over the speakerphone for the first time. Then he flew over, a day or two later, they came to my apartment and we worked for a few hours and read scenes which Sally put on tape and looked at later. Then Sally took us to a show called *Def Poetry Jam*, and she said, "The verse is really more like rap than Shakespeare, so think of it in that way." And the show was very much reflective of that quality, with all these wonderful young writers performing amazing rap poems. And Sally said, "Would you do the film?" because she'd watched the footage and she felt that the chemistry between Simon and I was right. And I felt that it was right, too.

Q: How did you find Simon Abkarian?

SP: Simon lives in Paris. He's worked a lot in the theatre, particularly with Ariane Mnouchkine and the Théâtre du Soleil.

He's performed the Greek tragedies, and Shakespeare, but before this film, he had done relatively little cinema. I first met him when he came to audition for a small part, as a gypsy, in *The Man Who Cried* and he made a big impression on me. When I started work on *YES* I remembered him for his charisma and his intensity, his intelligence and his presence. I asked him to come and read and thought he was quite, quite extraordinary. He has been a true and generous collaborator and companion throughout the development of the film and some parts of the narrative are based on stories he told me. This is his first lead role on film, and his first major role in the English language, which is an incredible, astonishing achievement.

By the way, Simon is in fact Armenian, but from Beirut. And we went to Beirut together to look for locations and to deepen my research; to help me understand the background of his character in the story. We were going to shoot there, but just as we started filming, America invaded Iraq and we couldn't get insurance to cover the cast and crew. And then the Bush administration created a decree which made it impossible for Joan to go to Cuba. And so at the last minute we ended up shooting Beirut in Cuba and parts of Cuba in the Dominican Republic. That's filmmaking for you.

Q: Can you talk about the character of the husband, played by Sam Neill?

SP: Sam tackled his part very courageously, because I think it's the most difficult part in the film. It's the apparently unsympathetic character, you know, the white, male, middle-aged man who's powerful, and who gets all the blame for everything. But we talked a lot about trying to find sympathy and compassion for the loneliness of that place and for his character, even though he may be doing and saying alienating things. There is a moment, for example, when he looks at himself in the mirror and talks about "the ache of emptiness" and of course there is his air-guitar solo, which reveals his hidden vulnerability and his crushed dreams of personal expression and freedom. I think we all felt very, very compassionate towards him. There are no bad characters in this story, as far as I'm concerned. They're just each in their own form of solitude or suffering.

Q: Could you talk about the cleaning ladies?

SP: It's a very old device. It's the chorus in Greek tragedy. In a way the cleaner is the intermediary between us and the characters, between our experience and the film. And she's also the invisible witness, you know, the one that isn't noticed, but who sees it all. I tried to give a voice to each character in different ways and for different reasons, but hers is a particular voice, and one that is rarely heard.

In writing her part I got really involved in the metaphysics of dirt and in the lives of the hidden army of those that clean up after us, in our homes and on the planet, from birth onwards; first our mothers and then others—unintentional rhyme! I felt more and more in awe, actually, of the unacknowledged and undervalued under-class of cleaners and decided to try and make one who was the true philosopher and scientist of the piece. Actually, I believe working people *are* scientists and philosophers, but without college degrees. Anyway, the cleaner is the one who is not seen, but who sees everything.

I also thought it was important that there was laughter in the film, and she is very funny. The deeper subject of East/West relations is so difficult and potentially heavy that to have levity and permission to laugh with it is a kind of necessary elixir.

Q: I saw a thank you to John Berger in the credits. Can you explain why?

SP: John Berger, for those of you who may not know him, is a great, great writer who was born in England and now lives in France. He wrote *G* and many other novels and is also very widely known as an art critic for his incredibly influential work, *Ways of Seeing*. He's a poet, too, and he combines a poetic sensibility with personal and political integrity, always speaking out what he believes, from the heart. I've been fortunate enough to get to know him. I was too shy to approach him for many, many years. I'd been a huge fan and admirer of his, but didn't dare to write to him. I thought, "Why would he want to hear from me?" And then he saw *The Tango Lesson* and wrote *me* a letter. I practically fell to the floor! Subsequently he has become both a friend and a mentor. He read several successive drafts of this script, and was very encouraging about it. And so my thanks are due to him and all like him, in this strange international kinship of soulmates that one somehow finds. I'm sure there are many of you out there.

Q: Were there any other thinkers and writers who inspired you?

SP: I think that the first writer who influenced this film was James Joyce. The title of the film is the last word of James Joyce's *Ulysses*, his great project of the stream of consciousness. I wanted similarly, to try to get inside my characters' heads and listen to what was there. I suppose I wanted to find some kind of cinematic equivalent to the stream of consciousness. In the end we spoke of the verse as a river! So Joyce was one major influence. But so were rap artists. And so were the cleaners that I've overheard talking to each other, and guys walking down the street saying fucking this and fucking that and fucking this and fucking that. I wanted to find a way of bringing the music and rhythms of the speech of everyday life onto the screen. Because none of the words that people use in the film are particularly long, academic, or complicated; it's very everyday speech; it's just how the words are arranged that is different.

Q: The scene in the car park, can you both talk about the creation of that from rehearsal into its final form on the screen?

JA: We rehearsed the scene in Sally's studio and then she would take Simon and me to different places and we would run the scene to see how it worked. In fact we went to three or four different car parks. The night when we finally filmed it was at the end of the shoot in London, right before we went to the Dominican Republic. Strangely, though I had felt so "in the zone" for the whole shoot, I didn't particularly feel "in the zone" that night. It seemed sort of problematic; the lights weren't really working, we were exhausted, we were all getting on a plane, like 24 hours later, but I think the exhaustion somehow was right. We had had a very emotional rehearsal of the scene around the table in rehearsal a few days before, where we all had cried a lot. We had talked about the various perspectives, like what they were each thinking and feeling and the frustration that they can't understand each other. We were all crying, and I think I had expected to try to get to that state again on the night we filmed it. And when it didn't happen, it ended up being the best thing. It was better that we did that around the table, rather than doing it in the actual scene. We had had the opportunity to go through it, and I think that although I wasn't very conscious of it, the exhaustion and the fragmented quality of the night lent itself to the scene, and underplaying some of the stuff was a lot better than going over the top with it. It was more effective.

SP: That's exactly right. Sometimes you have to shed the tears in advance and work through your own feelings about the material in order to achieve a certain kind of transparency when you shoot it; which I think is exactly what Joan and Simon did. And I think restraint is sometimes much, much more powerful, when you've worked something through, as we had, than over the top expression.

Q: I'm wondering about the scene when he goes back to Beirut. It felt like he had to return to his own roots before he could reach out to someone who had become the enemy. Is that right?

SP: One of the things that we talked about a lot in rehearsal, and also cried about together, actually, was the necessity to not only love, but also to respect difference. That means, of course, also accepting and taking responsibility for who and what you are. But the crucial element seems to be the act of listening, and in the act of listening to others, understanding where they are coming from. We talked a lot about this when we were working on the long car park scene.

And the notion of "the enemy" is a complicated one; historically we can see that it sometimes is an invention, a fiction, to justify the apparatus of war and to keep the population in a docile state of fear. One war after another also creates a huge mobile population where people have been traumatically torn from their roots and have become refugees. And I think that, in effect, each of the characters in the story is in their own kind of exile. All of us face the question of where "home" is, especially now that we live in a globalised economy. Perhaps we each have to find our own roots and know where we're coming from before we can disengage and not over-identify with the nationalist part of our identity, which ultimately divides us from others. Own it, love it, move on.

Q: I thank you from the bottom of my heart for showing us this work of art. And I ask you from the tip of my tongue, what advice you have for us directors who are young?

[AUDIENCE LAUGHTER]

SP: Don't give up. That's the first thing and the most important thing. Take risks. Don't play safe. Do what you really believe in; life is too short to do it for money or for anything else.

Cast and Crew Credits

GREENESTREET FILMS
AND
UK FILM COUNCIL
PRESENT

AN
ADVENTURE PICTURES
PRODUCTION

IN ASSOCIATION WITH
STUDIO FIERBERG

A FILM BY
SALLY POTTER

Y E S

Written and directed by
SALLY POTTER

Produced by
CHRISTOPHER SHEPPARD
ANDREW FIERBERG

Executive Producers
JOHN PENOTTI
PAUL TRIJBITS
FISHER STEVENS
CEDRIC JEANSON

JOAN ALLEN

SIMON ABKARIAN

SAM NEILL

SHIRLEY HENDERSON
SHEILA HANCOCK

SAMANTHA BOND
STEPHANIE LEONIDAS

GARY LEWIS
WIL JOHNSON
RAYMOND WARING

Director of Photography
ALEXEI RODIONOV

Editor
DANIEL GODDARD

Production Design
CARLOS CONTI

Costume Design
JACQUELINE DURRAN

Sound
JEAN-PAUL MUGEL
VINCENT TULLI

Casting
IRENE LAMB

Line Producer
NICK LAWS

CAST
(in order of appearance)

Cleaner. . . . . SHIRLEY HENDERSON
She . . . . JOAN ALLEN
Anthony . . . . SAM NEILL
He. . . . . SIMON ABKARIAN
Virgil. . . . . WIL JOHNSON
Billy. GARY LEWIS
Whizzer. . . . . RAYMOND WARING
Grace. . . . . STEPHANIE LEONIDAS
Cleaner in Swimming Pool . . . .
BARBARA OXLEY
Kate. . . . . SAMANTHA BOND
Waiter . . . . KEV ORKIAN
Kitchen Boss . . . . GEORGE YIASOUMI
Cleaner in Laboratory. . . . . . BERYL SCOTT
Aunt. . . . . SHEILA HANCOCK
Father Christmas . . . . LOL COXHILL
Priest. . . . . FATHER CHARLES OWEN
Nuns . . . . MANDY COOMBES
BETI OWEN
Cleaner in Nursing Home . . . . DOT BOND
Woman in Cuban Apartment . . . .
DORCA REYES SÁNCHEZ
Friends in Beirut . . ANTOINE AGOUDJIAN
CHRISTINA GALSTIAN

Associate Producers. . . . .
LUCIE WENIGEROVÁ
DIANE GELON

Production Manager . . . . MICHAEL MANZI

Script Supervisor. . . . . PENNY EYLES
Story Editor. . . . . WALTER DONOHUE
Production Coordinator. . SCOTT BASSETT
Second Assistant Director . . . .
OLIVIA PENISTON-BIRD
Director's Assistant . . . . AMOS FIELD REID
Production Assistants. . . . DAVID PURCHAS
HESTER CAMPBELL
Assistant to Joan Allen. . . . . PAM PLUMMER

Steadicam Operator . . . . ERIC BIALAS
Focus Puller / Operator . . DENIS GARNIER
Clapper Loader . . . . SARA DEANE
Boom Operator. . . . . PIERRE TUCAT

Chief Make-up Artist . . . .
CHANTAL LÉOTHIER

Stills Photographers . . . . . . NICOLA DOVE
GAUTIER DEBLONDE
Videographer. . . . . DANIEL MUDFORD

Production Lawyer. . . . .
LAW OFFICE DIANE GELON
Production Accountants . . PETER EARDLEY
FREYA PINSENT

LONDON CREW
Location Manager. . . . . . BEN GLADSTONE
Location Assistant. . . SAMSON HAVELAND
Casting Assistant . . . . EMILY CRAIG
Third Assistant Directors. . . . ADAM COOP
CHRISTOPHER BURGESS
Floor Runner. . . . . MICHAEL CLARK-HALL

Art Director . . . . CLAIRE SPOONER
Art Department Assistants. . . . .
JOSHUA HARTNETT
CESAR BAEZ

Set Costumer. . . . . CAMILLE BENDA
Additional Costumes . . . .
CARLO MANZI RENTALS
ANGELS THE COSTUMIERS

Wigs . . . . LONDON WIGS

Gaffers. . . . . MARK CLAYTON
BARNABY SWEET
Electrician. . . . . BENJAMIN KERR
Trainee Electrician . . . . XIAOYU LI
Trainee Clapper Loader . . . .
ANNA CARRINGTON

Catering . . 5 STAR LOCATION CATERING
Location Vehicles . . . . WILLIES WHEELS Ltd
Unit Driver. . . . . IAN LISI
Fight Coordinator . . . ANDREAS PETRIDES

CUBA CREW
Local Production . . AUDIOVISUALES ICAIC
PRODUCCIÓN-DISTRIBUCIÓN
Executive Producer . . . .
FRANK CABRERA RODE
Production Manager. . . . .
IOHAMIL NAVARRO CUESTA
Location Manager. . . . .
CARLOS DE LA HUERTA
Production Assistant. . . . .
JORGE GARCÍA LORENZO
Runners. . . . . ALBERTO REYTOR
MALVIN CABRERA
CARLOS CAMACHO
Accountant . . . . VIVIAN POMBO
Production Coordinator. . . . .
MIRIAM MARTÍNEZ
First Assistant Director . . . .
CARLOS BUSTAMANTE
Make-Up Artist . . . . MAGALY BATISTA
Casting Director. . . . . ALINA POMBO
Set Dresser. . . . . LIZ ALVAREZ
Translator. . . . . JULIO CÉSAR MORA
Wardrobe. . . . . ELBIA RONDÓN
Props . . . . RAFAEL SOUCHAY
Gaffer . . . . HUMBERTO FIGUEROA
Electricians. . . . . DANIEL PÉREZ
ARIEL LEYVA
Grip . . . . HECTOR ALFARO
Sunset Operator. . . . . . DAMIAN FUENTES
Production Drivers . . . . . JORGE MENDIVIL
ALEXANDER IBAÑEZ
Minibus Driver . . . . . . ARMANDO ROCHE

Crew and Cast Drivers . . . .
FRANCISCO CRUZ
NELSON HERNÁNDEZ
Production Van . . . . IGNACIO VALDÉS
Camera Truck Driver . . . .
LUCIDES COLLAZO
Grip Truck . . . . JULIO CRUZ
Lighting Truck . . . . RICARDO VICTORES
Genny Operators . . . MIGUEL MONTALVO
CARLOS MIRANDA

DOMINICAN REPUBLIC CREW
Local Production . . . . . BASANTA & Co, S.A.
Executive Producer . . . . . . JUAN BASANTA
Location Manager . . FERNANDO MEDINA
Production Manager . . . . PABLO LLUBERES
Production Assistants . . . . . ELENA TEJADA
JOSÉ ENRIQUE ESPÍRITU SANTO
Costumes . . . . CHELY MORAN
Art Department . . . . TANYA VALETTE
ISMAEL GUANTE
RAUL RECIO
Catering . . . . CLARA RODRIGUEZ
ORLANDO CARABALLO
Grips . . . . JULIO CÉSAR DIAZ V.
RADAMÉS REYES
JOSÉ MANUEL HERNÁNDEZ
MIGUEL TAPIA
Dolly Grip . . . .
ANDRÉS GONZÁLES "KABUBI"
Electricians . . . . FRANCISCO HERRERA
CRISTINO ADAMES
Transportation . . . . JOSÉ JIMÉNES
Dominican Casting . . . .
VOLUMEN AGENCIA DE CASTING

BELFAST CREW
Production Coordinator . . . DEAN HAGAN
Runner . . . . ROBERT WARD
Driver . . . . RAYMOND BURNS

BEIRUT CREW
Executive Producer . . . . . . MICHEL GHOSN
Production Manager . . . . LARA SABA
Armenian Advisor . . . . . HAGOP HANDIAN

POST-PRODUCTION CREW
Post-production Supervisor . . . .
JONATHAN HAREN
Post-production Consultants . . . .
JEANETTE HALEY
EMMA ZEE
Assistant Editors . . . . TOM KINNERSLY
ANJA SIEMENS
LALIT GOYAL
SEAN LYONS

Re-recording Mixer . . . . . . VINCENT TULLI
Assistant Re-recording Mixer . . . .
RICHARD STREET
Re-recorded at . . . SHEPPERTON STUDIOS

Sound Effects Editor . . . .
JOAKIM SUNDSTRÖM
Dialogue & ADR Editor . . . .
ANNE DELACOUR
Supervising Foley Editor & Mixer . . . .
ANTHONY FAUST A.M.P.S.
Foley Editor . . . . ROBERT BRAZIER
Foley Artist . . . . GEORGE HAPIG
ADR Mixer . . . . JEAN-PAUL MUGEL
Foley and ADR recorded at . . MAYFLOWER
STUDIOS
Dialogue Coaches . . POLL MOUSSOULIDES
JOAN WASHINGTON
Digital Colour and Visual Effects by . . . .
DIGIMAGE

Production Managers . . . .
TOMMASO VERGALLO
JUAN EVENO
ANGELO COSIMANO
Head of Technology . . . FRANÇOIS DUPUY
Digital Grading . . . . CLAIRE COUTELLE
Assisted by . . . . ALINE CONAN
NATACHA LOUIS
Scanning . . . . SILVAIN HEITZ
On-line Editing . . . . KENJI CHANSIN
CHRISTOPHE ROBLEDO
Digital Operator . . . .
JEAN RÉMY MORANÇAIS
Post Supervisor . . . . TOBY RIDGWAY

Scientific Images . . . .
OXFORD SCIENTIFIC FILMS

Research . . . . ANN HUMMEL

Avid supplied by . . . . ARTISTIC IMAGES
Lighting Equipment . . . . AFM LIGHTING
AFM Contact . . . . EDDIE DIAS
Insurance Services . . . .
AON / ALBERT G. RUBEN
Completion Bond. . . . FILM FINANCES LTD
For Film Finances . . . .
SHEILA FRASER MILNE
RUTH HODGSON
Freight Agent . . . .
DYNAMIC INTERNATIONAL
Rushes Processing . . . . SOHO IMAGES
Soho Images Liaison . . . MARTIN McGLONE
Negative Cutting . . . .
JASON WHEELER FILM SERVICES
Laboratory . . . . LABORATOIRE ÉCLAIR
Technical Director . . . PHILIPPE REINAUDO
Optical Grading . . . . BRUNO PATIN
Production Manager . . OLIVIER CHIAVASSA
Title Design . . . . STEPHEN MASTERS

Aaton Camera supplied by Ice Film

Film Stock supplied by Kodak

FOR GREENESTREET FILMS
Head of Production . . . . TIM WILLIAMS
Head of Business and Legal Affairs . . . .
VICKI CHERKAS
Manager of Business and Legal Affairs . . . . . .
MARY LAWLESS
Business and Legal Affairs Consultant . . . . . .
BRIAN KORNREICH
Assistant to John Penotti . . . . . LORI LAZAR
Assistant to Cedric Jeanson . . . .
MICHELLE JONAS

FOR UK FILM COUNCIL
Production Executive . . . . . EMMA CLARKE
Head of Physical Production . . . .
FIONA MORHAM
Senior Business Affairs Executive . . . .
NATALIE BASS

TEN LONG YEARS
Performed by B. B. King and Eric Clapton
Composed by Riley B. King/Jules Bihari
Careers – BMG Music Publishing (BMI)
Under license from
BMG Film & TV Music
Licensed courtesy of
Warner Strategic Marketing UK

WALTZ NO. 7 IN C SHARP MINOR
OP.64 NO.2
Composed by Frédéric Chopin
Performed by Dimitri Alexeev
Licensed courtesy of
EMI Records Ltd

CLAUDE CHALHOUB -
GNOSSIENNE
Performed by Claude Chalhoub
Composed by Eric Satie
(arr. by Claude Chalhoub)
with kind permission of Métisse Music (publisher)
(P) 2001 Teldec Classics International GmbH
Taken from the album Claude Chalhoub
8573-83039-2
Courtesy of Warner Classics

YEGHISHI BAR
Composed and performed by
Yeghish Manoukian
Courtesy of Parseghian Records

NORKETSOU BAR
Performed by Winds of Passion
Courtesy of Garni

FAWN
Composed by Tom Waits and
Kathleen Brennan
Arranged by Sally Potter and Fred Frith
© Jalma Music
By kind permission of
Warner/Chappell Music Limited

PIANO CONCERTO NO. 2
IN C MINOR, OP. 18
Composed by Sergei Rachmaninoff
Performed by Yefim Bronfman,

Courtesy of Boosey & Hawkes Licensing
Courtesy of Sony Classical
By arrangement with
Sony Music Licensing

WALTZ IN A FLAT MAJOR
Performed by Katia and
Marielle Labèque
Composed by Johannes Brahms
Courtesy of Sony Classical
By arrangement with
Sony Music Licensing

GLASS: PARU RIVER
By Philip Glass
Performed by Uakti
© 1999 Dunvagen Music
Publishers Inc
All rights reserved.
Used by permission.
Courtesy of The Decca Music Group Ltd
Licensed by kind permission from
The Universal Film & TV
Licensing Division

12/12
Performed by Kronos Quartet
Written by Ruben Isaac Alabarran Ortega
Enrique Arroyo, Jose Arrayo
and Emanuel Del Real Diaz
(arr. by Osvaldo Golijov)
Published by EMI Music Publishing
Licensed courtesy of
Warner Strategic Marketing UK

IGUAZU
Composed and performed by
Gustavo A. Santaolalla
Published by Universal /
MCA Music Ltd
Licensed courtesy of
Warner Strategic Marketing UK

EL CARRETERO
Composed by Guillermo Portabales
Arranged by Gonzalo Grau
© 1968 Peermusic (UK) Ltd.
Latin-American Music Pub. Co. Ltd

Original Music by. . . . . SALLY POTTER
With the participation of . . . . . FRED FRITH
Additional Arrangement . . . .
GONZALO GRAU
Music Consultant . . . . OSVALDO GOLIJOV
Music performed by:
Guitars. . . . . FRED FRITH
Cristal Baschet, Ondes Martenot . . . .
THOMAS BLOCH
Piano, Bass, Percussion . . GONZALO GRAU
Saxophone. . . . . THOMAS KOENIG
Trumpet. . . . . PHILIPPE SLOMINSKI
Duduk. . . . . ROSTOM KHACHIKIAN
Tres . . . . FINO GOMEZ ALMEIDA
Percussion. . . . . JEAN-PIERRE DROUET
Music recorded at . . . .
STUDIOS MERJITHUR, PARIS
Recording Engineer . . . . SAMY BARDET
Recording Supervisor. . . . FRANCK LEBON
Copyright Consultants . . . .
IVAN CHANDLER - MUSICALITIES
JILL MEYERS

With Special Thanks to
John Berger
and
Fiona Shaw

The Producers gratefully
acknowledge the contribution of:
Louis Bacon
Chris Pla
Michael Garfinkle
Michael Gordon
David Liptak
Joseph Petri
James Caccavo
Brian Collins

The Filmmakers wish to thank:
Philippe Akoka
Sandrine Ageorges
Beverly Berger
Nella Bielski
Gabriel Boustani
Giuliana Bruno
Amy Carr

Simon Channing Williams
Julie Christie
Eric Clapton
Prof. Shamshad Cockcroft
Prof. John Couchman
Robyn Davidson
Gail Egan
Roslyn Fierberg
Neil Gillard
Philip Glass
Kristina Goodman
Vince Holden
Amelia Hougen
Isaac and Mark
Achim Korte
Kronos Quartet
Pankaj Mishra
Prof. Peter Mobbs
Hinke Multhaupt
Jeannie Murphy
Thom Osborn
Leda Papaconstantinou
Simon Perry
Prof. Steven Rose
Gustavo Santaolalla
Catherine Schaub
Jean Turner
Tom Waits
Bart Walker

Frederick Sheppard (1920 – 2004)

Morris Fierberg (1930 – 2003)

The Advanced Biotechnology Centre,
Imperial College, London
Angie Bruce Flowers
Aquascutum
Staff and Residents of Athlone House
Nursing Home, Highgate
Autoridad Metropolitana de Transporte
(AMET)
Ayuntamiento de San Pedro de Macorís

Ayuntamiento Santo Domingo
Capital Scenery
Central Foundation Girls School, Bow
Cerruti
CXD
The Drapers' Company
Fornarina
Grahams Hi-Fi
Gran Car Company, Cuba
LA Fitness, Leadenhall Street
Oficina de Patrimonio Cultural, Dominican
Republic
Northern Ireland Film and Television
Commission
Smiths of Smithfield
St. Joseph's Church at Highgate
Therapy, Bishopsgate
Únion Árabe de Cuba

Made with the support of the National
Lottery through the UK Film Council's New
Cinema Fund.

About the Filmmaker

SALLY POTTER (writer/director) left school at sixteen to become a film-maker, joining the London Filmmakers Co-op and starting to make experimental short films. She later trained as a dancer and choreographer at the London School of Contemporary Dance, before cofounding Limited Dance Company with Jacky Lansley.

Potter went on to become an award-winning performance artist and theatre director, with shows including *Mounting, Death and the Maiden*, and *Berlin* (with Rose English). In addition, she was a member of several music bands (including FIG and The Film Music Orchestra) working as a lyricist and singer. She collaborated (as a singer-songwriter) with composer Lindsay Cooper on the song cycle *Oh Moscow* which was performed throughout Europe, Russia, and North America. (Her music work continued later when she co-composed with David Motion the soundtrack to *Orlando*, and created the score for *The Tango Lesson*. Her most recent music work is as producer and composer of the original tracks for *YES*.)

Potter returned to filmmaking with her short film *Thriller* (1979), which was a hit on the international festival circuit. This was followed by her first feature film, *The Gold Diggers* (1983), starring Julie Christie; a short film, *The London Story* (1986); a documentary series for Channel 4, *Tears, Laughter, Fears and Rage* (1986); and a programme about women in Soviet cinema, *I Am an Ox, I Am a Horse, I Am a Man, I Am a Woman* (1988).

The internationally acclaimed *Orlando* (1992) bought Potter's work to a wide audience. Starring Tilda Swinton, the film was based on Virginia Woolf's classic novel (adapted for the screen by Potter). In addition to two Academy Award nominations, *Orlando* won more than twenty-five international awards, including the "Felix," awarded by the European Film

Academy for the best Young European Film of 1993, and first prizes at St Petersburg, Thessaloniki, and other festivals.

Potter's next film was *The Tango Lesson* (1997, in which she also performed, with renowned tango dancer, Pablo Veron). First presented at the Venice Film Festival, the film was awarded the "Ombú de Oro" for Best Film at Mar del Plata Festival, Argentina, the SADAIC Great Award from the Sociedad Argentina de Autores y Compositores de Música, as well as receiving "Best Film" nominations from BAFTA and the US National Board of Review.

In 2000 she completed *The Man Who Cried* (starring Johnny Depp, Christina Ricci, Cate Blanchett, and John Turturro), a story set just before World War II in Paris, in the world of the opera.

Potter is also the author of the screenplay books *Orlando*, *The Tango Lesson*, and *The Man Who Cried*.